Hoofbeats

Katie and the Mustang

Book One

by KATHLEEN DUEY

PUFFIN BOOKS

PUFFIN BOOKS
Published by Penguin Group
Penguin Young Readers Group, 345 Hudson Street,
New York, New York 10014, U.S.A.
Penguin Books Ltd, 80 Strand, London WC2R ORL, England
Penguin Books Australia Ltd, 250 Camberwell Road,
Camberwell, Victoria 3124, Australia
Penguin Books Canada Ltd, 10 Alcorn Avenue,
Toronto, Ontario, Canada M4V 3B2
Penguin Books (N.Z.) Ltd, 182-190 Wairau Road,
Auckland 10, New Zealand

Published simultaneously in the United States of America by Dutton Children's
Books and Puffin Books, divisions of Penguin Young Readers Group, 2004

7 9 10 8 6

Puffin Books ISBN 0-14-240090-4

Printed in the United States of America

*My childhood memories are set to hoofbeats:
a fog-softened gallop on a lonely morning; the joyous
clatter of friends pounding down the Canal Road;
a measured, hollow clop of a miles-to-go July afternoon;
the snow-muffled hoofbeats of wintertime; the squelching
rhythm of a close race with a rainstorm. These books
are for my dear friends, the horses of my childhood—
Buck, Ginger, Steve, and Cherokee Star.*

Thank you all.

CHAPTER ONE

❧ ❧ ❧

The stinkweed made me sick. The two-leggeds who
drove me from my herd and my home starved me a long
time before I would eat it, but, in the end, I had no
choice. I am too sick and too weak to fight the ropes.
But the sickness will not last....

I was hiding from Mrs. Stevens that day. It was
cold in the barn, though not bitter, not too
bad for early February. We'd had one warm snap
that hatched a few flies, then it had stormed again.
There were dirty banks of snow along the roads.

I pulled my jacket tighter around my shoulders.
It was too big—it was a castoff from Mr. Stevens—
but my dress was getting too small. It was about
worn-out. The blue homespun was faded and
stained, and one sleeve had a long, mended tear.
I didn't care about any of that as much as the way
it pulled across my back.

It was just past sunrise. I had done my early chores—the milk was poured into the cooling can, the milk bucket washed. Mrs. Stevens insisted on that, every day. The minute the milk was poured out, the bucket had to be scrubbed with soap in the tin basin. Every two days, I had to change the wash water.

I sighed. I knew I should go back to the house and begin the real work of the day. I just didn't want to.

"My uncle Jack hasn't written me," I explained to Betsy. "But people say it can take a year or more." I smiled, remembering my tall, handsome Uncle Jack with his dark hair and light blue eyes—and his grin.

I took a long breath, and my dress rubbed against the welts on my back. They weren't that bad; in a few days they'd be gone. But they hurt. My throat ached, and then, all of a sudden, my eyes stung. I pressed my lips together, hard. I did not want to cry. No amount of tear shedding was going to change Mrs. Stevens's temperament.

She had willow-switched me the day before . . . she was convinced I'd taken a spoon from her mother's silver service set. I hadn't. What would I want with a spoon?

Hiram Weiss was the only other possible suspect, though, and no one would ever think he had taken it. I liked Hiram. He didn't talk very much, but he always nodded and smiled at me. He was from back east somewhere. Mrs. Stevens had told me he'd had some bad luck back there. She hadn't said more. I think she didn't know anything more. Hiram was tight-lipped. But everyone liked him; no one bothered him. He was as big as they come—broad and tall and heavy—plenty old enough to have a wife and children, but didn't have either. Mrs. Stevens always complained of the amount he ate at her table—but not to his face. Good farmhands were not so easy to find with everyone at loose ends deciding to pick up and go west.

"I'm sure Mrs. Stevens lost her own ding-dang spoon," I said. I took a breath and opened my mouth to tell Betsy more about it, to tell her how Mrs. Stevens had scowled at me when I insisted I hadn't taken anything of hers, how she had sent me down to the creek to cut the willow switch. But that wasn't what came out. What came out was this:

"It was all over in three weeks."

Betsy wasn't looking at me as I spoke. She never

did. I cleared my throat. "The fever was wildfire fast. Everyone says so."

I paused while the familiar pain in my throat got worse. I couldn't even whisper the rest of it, about the fever that had taken Mama and Pa and Tess. It had been almost three years ago, and I could still barely even *think* it. I longed to wake up one morning and have it not be true. But every morning I woke up—and it was.

Betsy shifted her weight. She turned her head to look at me, chewing her cud. Then she switched her ropy tail and stamped one hind hoof. A half-dozen chilly flies rose an inch from the straw, then settled again. They were too cold to fly any farther. I pulled in a long, slow breath of barn dust and hay smell.

"On the funeral day," I said quietly, "I just sat in the parlor while neighbor women fussed over the food."

I stopped to breathe in and out slowly, long enough to keep myself from crying. Then I went on. "Mrs. O'Reilly, Mrs. Gleason, and Mrs. Wittmann came from their farms. I hated the smell of their cooking in Mama's kitchen. I just hated them for being in there at all." I tacked the last part on in a near whisper.

I had been six years old when the fever hit. Mrs. O'Reilly, Mrs. Gleason, and Mrs. Wittmann: I could barely picture their faces now—nor the faces of their children—even though I had gone to church with all of them. I hadn't seen any of them even once since that day. The Stevenses were not Irish nor Catholic—they weren't anything at all. So we never went to the little church that had no priest but still held prayer meetings.

I looked out the big double doors at the shade tree outside and sighed. I was twenty miles or more from my parents' farm in Cedar County. I had never asked to go back, and Mr. Stevens had never offered to take me. But Mama and Pa and Tess were buried on a ridge behind the house my father had built. So maybe the farm I had been born on still belonged to my family. In a way, maybe it was still my real home.

I cried a little. I was used to crying. But then I hushed so I could listen for the sound of the front door. If Mrs. Stevens caught me idling, she'd make me scrub down her porch floors with sand, or lime the privy, or something just as bad.

When I had first come, she had often twisted a strand of my hair around her finger and smiled, saying it was the color of fresh field corn. But things had changed within a month. I had never been able to figure out why. Maybe she had thought I would think of her as my mother—she had no children of her own. But I didn't. I couldn't. My mother had laughed all the time. She had enjoyed sunrise and making bread and playing with my sister and me.

After that first month, Mrs. Stevens seemed angry with me most of the time. It was even worse now. After my last bath she had all but pulled my tangled curls out of my scalp, she had brushed my hair that hard.

"I was so relieved when Mr. Stevens said he'd take me in," I whispered to Betsy. "I was so afraid no one would—all the closest neighbors had big families they could barely feed. I know they all thought this was best for me, but now..."

The old cow flopped her ears and stared at nothing, her jaw working steadily. She was a Jersey milker and she had a simple life. Daytime was for eating, nights were for sleeping. She stood still when I milked her morning and evening. She was glad to see me when her bag was full and heavy. In between, she paid less attention to me than a tree stump would have. Sometimes I envied her.

I sighed. The horses were more polite about listening, but they were all out of the barn this morning. Mr. Stevens had hitched Delia and Midnight to the buggy and gone to town, and Hiram had the draft horses dragging the sledge over the half-frozen ground down by the creek.

Last year's cornstalks were still standing, dried and brown—Mr. Stevens had let them go last fall because of an early wet spell. Hiram Weiss had said once that Mr. Stevens hated farming. He surely wasn't very good at it. Yet he always seemed to have money, and I wondered more than once where it came from.

Hiram was a grand farmer, but he didn't have his own farm any more than I did. He told me once that New York City, where he'd lived for a while, was full of people who couldn't find enough work to eat and that Scott County, Iowa, was a paradise compared to what was going on back there.

I liked Hiram. He had first come around asking

for work the year before the fever took my family. He reminded me a little of my father, but younger. Pa was quiet, but he liked to hear other people talk about when to plant and how to store grain and everything in between. My mother had liked cooking for guests when we had enough to go around. So we'd had neighbors sitting on our porch once or twice a month—whenever anyone came by our place on their way to Davenport for dry goods or salt or to visit the courthouse.

Mrs. Stevens almost never had a caller. Mr. Stevens got in the buggy and went visiting on his own whenever he needed a conversation—sometimes he went all the way to Davenport—but he almost never took his wife. And I was sure he never once thought about taking me along, even though he knew I had written five letters to my uncle Jack over the past year and desperately wanted an answer to arrive at the Davenport post office. Mr. Stevens barely noticed me unless I did something wrong.

"I'll milk early tonight if I can," I said to Betsy. She flicked one floppy funnel-shaped ear.

I heard a familiar mewling behind me as I picked up the milk bucket. I glanced over my shoulder and made my voice sound like I was astonished. "Tiger? What do you want? Milk?" Tiger didn't understand the joke.

The cat stretched, arching her back and her long tail. She listened to me sometimes, but only so long as I scratched her ears. If I stopped, she would stalk away, her knees stiff and her tail twitching.

"Katie!"

I jumped, my heart slamming at my ribs.

Mrs. Stevens has a voice like a branch scraping a tin roof when she raises it to shout—and she sounded close. She was coming up the barn path. Why hadn't I heard the front door shut?

I smoothed my dress where it hung below my coat, trying to think what excuse I might give. I had finished hanging the laundry and had split stove-wood for the next day an hour quicker than usual just to warm myself up. But that wouldn't matter. Here I was, sitting idle and with nowhere to hide.

"Katie Rose!"

I stood up and ran three steps to snatch a pitch-fork from its wall hooks. It was a silly ruse. Hiram kept the stalls clean and the aisles swept. What chore could I pretend to be doing with a pitchfork?

But then the door swung wide; I blinked at the sudden glare. There was an old, spreading ash tree outside, but the shade was broken by a shaft of early morning sunlight. With the sun behind her, Mrs. Stevens looked golden, like an angel. Then she stepped inside the dim barn, and she was a pinch-mouthed farmwife again.

"Katie! Whatever do you *do* out here?"

I knew better than to answer. Any explanation would be the wrong one, especially the truth. Talking to a cow?

"I asked you a question." Mrs. Stevens put her hands on her hips.

I just stood there, my eyes down.

Mrs. Stevens sighed. "Daydreaming and mooning again? Do you think that'll get the chores done? Perhaps a few hours of real work would cure you of idleness. Or maybe a long stand in the corner."

My whole body went stiff. I hated standing in the corner worse than extra chores or even getting a whipping. She knew it.

Mrs. Stevens suddenly tilted her head. "Oh my," she breathed. "He's early."

Then I heard it, too: faint hoofbeats and the distant grating of metal-shod cartwheels. Mr. Stevens was coming home.

Mrs. Stevens had turned to face the barn door. Now she spun around and made a motion like she was shooing hens. "Hurry!"

I almost smiled. I was afraid of her. But she was afraid of him. Mr. Stevens never struck his wife, but he shouted and cursed sometimes if he saw her idle. And he took pride in her never talking back to him, ever. I had heard him brag about it to Hiram. When he shouted at Mrs. Stevens, she would shrink in on herself for days afterward. But she never seemed angry at him, only at herself—and me.

"Sssst!" Mrs. Stevens hissed again, glaring. "Come on, girl, come on!"

"Yes, ma'am," I answered, still fighting the smile. She was whispering as though her husband, still a half mile away, could somehow hear her.

I leaned the pitchfork against the wall and followed her along the lilac hedge, down into the yard. The dogs were milling at our feet, and Mrs. Stevens shut them up in their pen. "Get the rug beaters!" she ordered over her shoulder. Her voice was even sharper than usual. I set the milk bucket inside the back door and ran for the pantry closet.

By the time the cart clattered around the spring-house, we were both beating the rugs she had hung on the fence two days before to air, the beater wires humming. I hated this chore. I always coughed the whole time, breathing the fine grayish dust. The spring-wire handle of the beater was freezing cold, and it rubbed hard on my palm, but it didn't hurt anymore. I had grown calluses for it. What hurt were the willow-switch stripes on my back where my dress pulled across my skin.

Mrs. Stevens beat her rugs four times a year. She loved them. They were ugly, I thought, dark red with big white and black diamond shapes around the edges. But the wool was still thick and tight. They had been her grandmother's, brought all the way from England seventy years before.

I had once spilled milk on the edge of the biggest one. Mrs. Stevens's face had turned the color of her precious rugs. She had scolded me like a mean dog growls, standing within an inch of my nose, shaming me for ruining what the women in her family had kept stainless for three generations. I knew why the rugs had lasted that long. Her grandmothers had probably been strict and mean and had company only once or twice a year, just like her. The Stevens house was as quiet as midnight most the time.

"Mind you, do it in a circle pattern," Mrs. Stevens scolded me lightly.

She had it all figured out. The best way to knock dust and dirt out of a rug was to hit it in a rapid circle that got wider and wider as you went around it. It seemed silly to me.

I looked up. The carriage was nearly to the yard drive.

"See that you keep beating," Mrs. Stevens warned me.

"I will," I promised, and waited until she had walked away to angle my body so I could wallop the blasted rug and watch the cart approach at the same time.

The buggy team was trotting, Mr. Stevens's string-leather whip popping above their backs. I loved to watch the mares, their knees and fetlocks snapping up and down, as regular as the beat of a duck's wings. Their manes flew out behind as the road angled and they crossed the breeze.

It was then that I noticed. Tied behind the cart

was a horse I had never seen before. He was the color of dark honey, with a mane and tail as black as midnight. He ticked a front hoof and stumbled, then caught his stride again as Mr. Stevens reined the mares in. Mrs. Stevens walked to meet the wagon. I stood still, beating the rug, watching.

Mr. Stevens set the brake handle and climbed down, stiff and gimpy from the long ride. He was smiling, though. He pointed at the horse. "He's a Mustang, fresh broke in, and I got him cheap. He needs feeding up."

Mrs. Stevens nodded cautiously.

Mr. Stevens was standing tall, his collar buttoned high. He laid one finger on his cheek, something he often did when he was about to say something he thought truly important. "Mustangs make fine saddle horses," he announced, "if a man can handle them."

"Mustangs?" Mrs. Stevens spat out the unfamiliar word like it tasted sour.

Mr. Stevens glanced past her and noticed me. "Haven't you got something to do?"

I realized I had stopped beating the rug and started up again.

"Go see if there are more eggs for supper," Mrs. Stevens shouted at me. "And mind you don't bother the broody hen!"

Glad to be done with the cloud of rug dust, I hung the beater on its nail by the back door, glancing back over my shoulder every few seconds.

Mr. Stevens had untied the Mustang stallion and was leading him toward the barn. He was the most beautiful horse I had ever seen, even though he was too thin—his sides were ridged by his ribs. He looked young, but he walked like an old pasture mare, aged past having colts or doing buggy work, scuffing the toe of each hoof in the dust.

At the barn door, the stallion hesitated. He tossed his head, and the sunlight caught his dark gold coat, glinting like kindling sparks. Mr. Stevens jerked the lead rope. The stallion stepped forward into the barn, and the sparks went out.

CHAPTER TWO

❧ ❧ ❧

The ropes and whips and the shouts have taken
everything from me. My mares are gone. The smell of
sagebrush and rain, the mountains that guided my way, are
far behind. I hate the two-leggeds for chasing me across
the plains, for making me come so far toward the rising sun.
And I hate the wooden box that traps me here.

I was startled out of my dreams by the dogs barking. I sat up on my pallet, blinking in the dark for a few seconds. Then I pushed my mother's book into its hiding place beneath my blankets and stood up.

"Hiram! Get up!" It was Mr. Stevens's voice, screaming the command like he was talking to a dog.

It was dark, but I found the door handle easily enough—without taking a single step. I didn't have a proper room to sleep in, but Mrs. Stevens had given me her biggest closet—an old pantry she rarely used since they had built their springhouse.

"Hiram!"

Hiram slept in an old pig shed. He had it all cleaned up and decent inside—I peeked in it once when he was gone. He worked part-time on the Stevens farm and part-time for whichever neighbors needed help. If he worked more than a mile or two away, he'd take his bedroll and sleep over. He came and went without my knowing. Unless I paid attention, I never knew whether he was on the place or not.

"Can you see what's wrong yet?" That was Mrs. Stevens. She wasn't exactly shouting, but she had raised her rough voice to a high pitch so it would carry through the dogs' racket. It sounded like she was standing by the front door—or maybe just outside, on the planked porch.

"Mr. Stevens?" she called.

No answer.

"Robert?" she pleaded. "Are you all right?"

Using his given name didn't help a bit. Her husband didn't answer her. "Hiraaaam!" he shouted once more, dragging the name out like a coyote howl.

"Should I dress?" Mrs. Stevens beseeched her husband. "Should I dress and come out there? Do you need help?"

Mr. Stevens ignored her again. I was pretty sure he couldn't hear her at all. The dogs were having conniption fits.

My clothes were laid over the back of a chair just outside my pantry as usual. I felt for them in the dark. I couldn't light a candle or Mrs. Stevens would scold me about wasting her tallow.

I pulled my nightshirt off and replaced it with my camisole, then stepped into my petticoat and dress. I tied the strings on my bodice with trembling fingers. Then I pulled on my shoes, wriggling my toes to straighten the wads of tissue paper in the toes. It was bound to be cold outside. Then I just stood there, shivering in the dark.

There was no scent of smoke—so there was no fire. But something was terribly wrong. Mr. Stevens would not be shouting like this over a fox in the yard.

"Hiram!"

His shouts were getting farther away.

I tiptoed out into the kitchen and bent to look

out the window. Mr. Stevens was carrying a lantern. I could see the yellowish glow sliding over the lilac hedge as he walked up the path toward the barn.

Mrs. Stevens had ventured out into the house yard and was holding her bedroom candleholder, standing near the chicken coop.

There was a cascade of hen noise, and she stepped back a few paces.

"Hiram, raise yourself!" Mr. Stevens bellowed. He was halfway up the path.

"Coming!" came an answer at last. I was glad. No matter what was wrong, Hiram Weiss was a steady man, the kind of man my father would have liked.

Once Mr. Stevens stopped shouting, the yard dogs quieted some. It was then, for the first time, that I heard what had set them off. There was a muffled banging coming from the direction of the barn.

It was the stallion, kicking at the stall planks. What else could it be? The buggy team didn't have it in them to attack the wooden planks that held them from grazing on the new green grass when they wanted to.

Hiram shouted something I couldn't understand,

and I fidgeted. What would Mr. Stevens do to the horse? I knew I shouldn't leave the house without asking Mrs. Stevens, but I knew just as well that if I asked, she would forbid me to go at all. And, as usual, she would get angry at me, instead of at her husband.

The reason she was standing in the yard in her wrapper instead of dressing and running to help was that she knew her husband would be upset since he hadn't *told* her to come. I felt sorry for her. She spent half her time guessing what he wanted of her— and usually guessed wrong.

I grabbed my jacket from the hook, and moved a hat to cover its emptiness. Pulling it on, I went out the back door, opening and closing it in quick swooshes. The hasps were well oiled; squeaks bothered Mr. Stevens.

It was a dark night. The moon wasn't up yet. I crawled through the lilac hedge, then ran on the far side of it, half bent over, until I got well clear of the yard. I could hear the men shouting at the stallion.

I ran up the path toward the barn door. The dogs were still barking a little, but unless someone let them out of their pen, they knew their job was done. I had the hedge between me and the chicken coop. I could hear worry clucks inside, but no more than that. I was glad. Broken eggs and ruined chicks would only cause more trouble in the house.

Mr. Stevens had hung his lantern from one of the iron spikes driven into the wall of the barn. I stayed outside, just beyond the pale amber light, standing in front of the ash tree, hidden by the darkness but still able to see in through the open door.

The Mustang stallion was rearing, crashing his hooves on the top rail of his stall, dancing backward, then rearing again.

"Giddown, you crazy fool!" I couldn't see Hiram, but that was him, his voice calm but loud.

"Get back!" Mr. Stevens yelled. "He'll break out of there any second."

Hiram laughed. "No, no he can't. That's good thick wood, that rail."

The stallion reared again, then again. Hiram came into sight, the long buggy whip in one hand.

I flinched when I heard the first pop.

The stallion squealed, baring his teeth; he reared again.

The whip popped again, and the Mustang slewed sideways, his ears tight against his head.

He plunged in a circle, then stood at the back of the stall, his head high, his nostrils wide.

"There now, you settle down," Hiram said gently. "It's all right now. See?" Hiram added, looking at Mr. Stevens. "Something scared him is all."

"Well done," Mr. Stevens said.

Hiram chuckled. I could just see the side of his face. He was breathing hard, but he was smiling. "I didn't touch him with it. Just the noise to startle him. He learns fast."

Mr. Stevens came to stand beside Hiram. "He surely does, Hiram," he was saying. "When someone makes him learn."

I watched him take the whip from Hiram and approach the stall. He leaned over the rail and slashed it across the Mustang's face. I cried out, but neither of them noticed because the Mustang squealed, a long, high-pitched sound of rage. Then he exploded and lunged forward, teeth bared, slamming against the stall gate.

Mr. Stevens stumbled, his coat sleeve catching for an instant on the splintery rail. Hiram leapt forward and grabbed his collar, dragging him backward. He steadied Mr. Stevens for a second before he let go. He looked disgusted. "And now you teach him that you hit him no matter what he does!"

I watched Mr. Stevens square his shoulders as he faced Hiram. "I taught him to leave my stall rails in one piece; that's what I taught him," he said coldly. "The horse trader said a man has to be tough with these wild ones, has to let them know who is boss."

I watched Hiram, one hand over my mouth to keep from making more noise. Hiram pressed his lips together, his cheeks flushed. He was angry. And he was right. It didn't make any sense. If the horse was startled with the whip for rearing and then actually *whipped* for standing quietly, how would it ever figure out what Mr. Stevens wanted it to do?

I stared at the Mustang horse. It looked more sad than angry now, standing as far back against the wall as it possibly could. I could see a long whip welt on its neck and another across its muzzle that was bleeding.

"With any luck, he'll settle until sunrise," Mr. Stevens said.

Hiram made a sound that could have been taken for anything—yes, no, or maybe so. Mr. Stevens raised the whip high over his head and slapped the lash across the stall rail. "You try to break down my barn like that again, and I'll show you what for," he said in a low, threatening voice. The Mustang lifted its head and flattened its ears.

Mr. Stevens hung up the whip, and, before I had time to think, he was walking toward the door—toward *me.* I froze, sure he would see me any second.

"I'll get him another bucket of water," I heard Hiram saying.

Mr. Stevens turned. I ran a few steps into the dark, dodging around the wide trunk of the ash tree. When I peeked out, he was frowning. I shivered from the cold and my own nervousness.

"No," he said. "He knocked it over. Teach him a lesson. Don't fill it until tomorrow night."

Hiram made another one of his yes-no-maybe-so sounds.

Mr. Stevens stepped out the door, and I crouched

behind the tree and waited until he had passed. Hiram was a few seconds behind him. I heard the barn door close, the hasps creaking under the weight. I sat pressed against the smooth gray bark, listening as Hiram's heavy footsteps faded, veering off behind the house, headed back toward the shed where he slept. I heard the chickens rustle and cluck as Mr. Stevens passed them, heard the front door open and close.

Then there was only the sound of frogs in the pond, croaking. One of the dogs yipped. I knew I should run for the back door. Now. I should have gone before Mr. Stevens had headed back toward the house. If he opened the door to the pantry where my pallet was and found it empty... But I didn't run. I stood there, staring at the closed barn door.

I bit my lip. It was Wednesday morning, even though it was still dark out. Was Mr. Stevens talking about not giving the horse any water until *Thursday* night? Two long days without water? I just couldn't walk away. The poor horse was so skinny... and so scared and miserable.

I could see the kitchen window over the lilacs.

There was no light inside. Mrs. Stevens had probably gone back to bed when the shouting was over—and Mr. Stevens had put the lantern out.

I shifted my weight back and forth, trying to decide. I might very well end up with another willow switching if they caught me outside without permission. But if they didn't actually see me, I was safe. Hiram wouldn't tell; he'd be glad the horse had gotten water after all. Hiram liked horses and cows and dogs and cats. He even liked pigs.

There was a quiet nickering from inside the barn. I had heard other horses make that sound. The Stevenses' plow team had been raised together—I don't think they had ever been apart. When one of the broad-backed draft horses was out in the pasture, and the other in the barn for some reason, they nickered back and forth like that—a soft, hopeful questioning sound.

I knew what it meant. The stallion was wondering if he had a friend anywhere nearby. I glanced once more at the house. I couldn't see even the faintest candlelight through the windows. The dogs had all gone quiet. The crickets in the lilacs were starting back up.

I bit my lip again. The Stevenses rarely checked on me once I was in the pantry and safely put to bed. If they hadn't already, they most likely wouldn't tonight. I counted to fifty. No one shouted from the house.

Shivering again, I ran to the barn door and unlatched it. I pulled the door open just wide enough to slip inside. I didn't want to light a lantern, but I had no choice if I was going to get the stallion a fresh bucket of water. It took me three tries to get the striker to work, but once I managed that, the wick lit right up. The sharp smell of oily lantern soot stung my nose and eyes.

I got a clean bucket from the tack room and walked to the well to fill it, keeping my skirt between the lantern and the front windows of the house. Then I set it low, behind the circle of stones around the mouth of the well. The rope slithered down silently, and the winch barely creaked as I raised the dripping bucket back up.

Carrying it slowly so it wouldn't slosh and soak my clothes, I got back inside as quick as I could and hung the lantern on a spike.

The stallion was still standing at the back of his

stall. His nostrils were no longer flared, though, and his ears were tipped toward me when I came in.

I brought the lantern closer to the stall. The empty bucket was on its side, just inside the gate, a few shards from the thin skin of ice on the water scattered beside it.

I slid the gate bar aside and took a deep breath. Probably best to do it fast. I leaned in to grab the bucket bale, snatching it toward me and shutting the gate all in one quick motion.

Then I looked back into the stall. The stallion hadn't moved. I did the same with the fresh bucket of water, placing it just inside, then ducking back out to slide the bar that locked the stall gate. The Mustang watched me.

"Are you a better listener than Betsy?" I asked him, nearly whispering. I winced, looking at the welts. "I'd rub some comfrey salve into those if I thought you'd let me."

The horse let out a long breath and then jerked his head up. His ears were flat again. I stepped back. "I won't try, I promise," I began, feeling foolish—surely he hadn't really understood. Then I heard a rustling in the straw and whirled around, afraid that

I had been caught after all. But it was the barn cat.

"That's just Tiger," I told the stallion. She mewed at the sound of her name and stretched, arching her back. There were flecks of straw in her dark, striped coat.

The stallion backed up, his eyes rimmed in white. He snorted and pawed at the ground as Tiger padded toward me, her eyes on the fresh water.

Suddenly, it all made sense. I had seen Tiger drink from the stock buckets a hundred times. She had gone into the Mustang's stall in the dark. Why not? The carriage team and the plow horses barely noticed her. But this wild horse had probably never seen a farm cat. And in the dark...

"Does Tiger smell like a mountain lion to you?" I whispered. Then I bent to intercept Tiger. She dodged around me and ran. I chased her across the dusty floor. She thought it was a game, and it took me a minute to get hold of her.

The stallion snorted and pawed as I swooped Tiger up. I carried her tight against my chest. "She can sleep with me tonight," I promised the Mustang. "I'll keep her in."

Then I blew out the lantern and closed the door.

The half-frozen soil crunched under my shoes as I walked back toward the house. Halfway there, I heard the Mustang nicker, asking that same soft question of the darkness.

CHAPTER THREE

🐎 🐎 🐎

The little one with the long mane smells good,
like bruised flowers. The old male who brings pain
and noise has not come again. Perhaps he is like a wolf
and won't come again until he is very hungry.
I must escape before then.

A week later, at breakfast, Mr. Stevens turned toward me and stared into my eyes. "My wife tells me she caught you in the barn again yesterday instead of doing your chores. That true?"

I swallowed a mouthful of boiled oats and lowered my eyes. It was. I had been out to the barn every time I got a chance. The Mustang was calmer. He didn't mind it when I walked by the stall now. And he usually whickered when I left.

"Well?" Mr. Stevens demanded.

I heard Mrs. Stevens clear her throat, and I

glanced at her. She was smiling slightly, as though the scolding pleased her.

Hiram, as always, acted as though he couldn't hear, forking down his eggs and bacon.

"I want you to stay out of the barn from now on," Mr. Stevens said sternly.

"She has to milk," Mrs. Stevens reminded him.

Mr. Stevens shot her an angry look. "Of course. I know that."

I sat very still, knowing that anything I said would only make things worse. Sometimes they seemed to use me as a way to be angry with each other.

"I meant except for the milking," Mr. Stevens said to me, daubing at his lips with his napkin. "She knew I meant that," he added, glancing at his wife, then back at me. "Didn't you, girl?"

I lowered my eyes instantly and nodded without looking at either one of them. I had learned to let them say whatever they cared to say without arguing, pretending not to be upset.

Hiram was finishing up his last bite of eggs. When he pushed back his plate, Mr. Stevens looked at him. "Hitch up the buggy team first today."

Hiram stood. Without anyone seeing, he gently

brushed the top of my head with his hand as he reached to gather up his plate and cup. Then, making one of his yes-no-maybe-so sounds as a response to Mr. Stevens, he carried his plate to the sideboard, winked at me, then went out the front door.

I stole a look at Mr. Stevens. He was nearly finished. I could barely wait for him to wipe his hands on his napkin and stand up to leave. I wanted to get out to the barn. I would milk Betsy fast as anything, then I could give the Mustang some oats and make sure his water bucket was full.

"We start spring cleaning next week on wash day," Mrs. Stevens said quietly.

I looked up. Spring cleaning already? It was barely February. Usually she waited until mid-April. "So early?" I asked quietly.

"Yes," Mr. Stevens said. "I have a cousin coming from Indiana in a few weeks." He narrowed his eyes, then went back to his oats, drizzling a little more honey into his bowl. He had a way of slurping up the cream that made my stomach uneasy. Several long minutes crept past. I kept chewing, fiercely, wanting only to be away from them both. I tipped my bowl to get the last of the oats onto my spoon. I had learned not to ask for seconds.

"You come in the minute you're finished with Betsy," Mr. Stevens warned me as he pushed his bowl away and picked up his empty coffee mug. "We don't feed and clothe you so you can loll around reading from that silly book."

I pressed my lips together. Was that how he imagined my days? All I ever did was work. I was so angry that I couldn't pretend hard enough. I frowned, and he saw it.

He ticked the edge of the cup with one thumbnail. "I'll take the book away if you disobey."

I dropped my spoon and it clunked on the floor, spattering the gluey oats in a little circle around it. I bent to pick up the spoon, wiping at the plank with my hand.

For some reason this struck him funny, and he laughed, then covered his mouth with his napkin. He stood up and went to the stove to refill his coffee cup.

I sat still, biting my lip. That book was *mine.*

Mr. Stevens went through the front door, walking out into the near dark. I knew what he would do. He would stand and sip his coffee until the sun came up. Then he'd be off somewhere. It was getting so Hiram did all the work on the farm.

"Put your dish in the basin," Mrs. Stevens said mildly. "Then wipe up the mess on the floor and go get that cow milked."

I stood up from the table and carried my bowl and spoon to the sideboard. Now that Mr. Stevens was gone, it was harder to pretend. My hands were shaking. When had he seen my book? I had never showed it to him. Mrs. Stevens had caught me reading it twice—but it had been at night, not when I was supposed to be working. She had mostly been angry about the candle stubs I had used to read. She must have told him about it.

I wet a rag in the washbasin and used it to wipe the floor. Then I pulled on my jacket and banged out the back door, starting up the hill in the gray dawn dusk.

Mr. Stevens had his back to me, standing by the buggy in the road. Hiram was there, too, and they were talking. I hurried up the path, keeping my head turned because I couldn't seem to stop the tears running down my face. I had gotten so good at pretending, but this morning, for some reason, I just couldn't manage it.

I knew why. The book was all I had. It was the only thing that had belonged to my mother that hadn't been sold off by the bankers. They had sold everything they could find, trying to get their money on my parents' debt—then they had sold the land itself.

No one had wanted to take me in. Everyone had been afraid of the fever—I couldn't blame them for that. In a way, I was grateful. For the better part of three weeks after the funeral services, I had been at the farm alone, taking flowers up to the graves, feeding the stock, cooking for myself.

One of the bank men had known about the Stevenses, that they had no children of their own, and he had arranged my coming here. Before the first sale, I hid two things: the book my mother had had since she was a girl and my father's silver shoe buckles.

I leaned on the ash tree by the barn door and forced myself to stop crying. Pa had been so proud of the silver buckles. They had been handed down from his great-grandfather. He had worn them every Sunday, fastened over his worn black shoes.

I wiped at my eyes with my sleeve and dragged in one long breath after another. Crying wasn't going to help anything. It never had. The buckles were wrapped in a tea cloth and buried beneath the lilac hedge. My book was beneath my pallet. Mr. Stevens was not going to get hold of either one.

I squared my shoulders and banged open the barn door, then stopped dead, standing just inside it, feeling foolish. I had startled the Mustang awake. He reared, then lashed out, his hooves striking the stall rails.

"Easy, easy," I pleaded with him. I leaned back to glance toward the house. Mr. Stevens couldn't help but hear. He was already upset with me. A commotion would make him furious.

"It's all right," I repeated over and over, quietly, standing very still. I could barely see in the near dark inside the barn. I heard the stallion drop back onto all four hooves. He was breathing hard.

I did not move an inch. "I never meant to scare you," I told him. "Please settle down. It's all right." I had heard my father calm farm horses with words like that all my life. He hadn't owned a horse whip.

"Just be easy and I'll get you some grain," I told him. I took one step into the dim barn. "All right? Just stand easy. Everything is all right. Just stand nice and easy."

My eyes were adjusting. The stallion snorted. I could just see his shape in the dim light coming through the wide door. His mane was so long and so matted. I took one more step. He stood still. He had been getting used to me, a little more each day, and now I had ruined everything. I saw him toss his head again. "You need a currycomb," I said quietly. The stallion reared and squealed softly.

I held my breath a moment; there were no shouts, no sound of footfalls on the path. Maybe Mr. Stevens and Hiram were talking and they hadn't heard anything. I knew I should milk quickly and get back down to the house. I would just do what I had gotten so good at with the Stevenses. I would act as though I was fine, that they hadn't scared me or upset me at all—but I would hide my book somewhere safe just in case.

"Listen," I told the Mustang, "you have to learn. Mr. Stevens scares me, too. But I learned to pretend."

The stallion was staring at me now, his neck arched. His breathing slowed a little. He didn't move as I came forward another step. When I lit the lantern, he reared, but his front hooves barely left the stall floor, and he didn't kick at the stall rails. He danced in a circle, and, as always, I was amazed at how agile he was, how he seemed to know exactly how big the stall was. He missed hitting the rails by inches.

"Perfect," I murmured. "You'd do fine at a barn dance." I took the milk pail off the hook and moved very slowly toward Betsy's stall at the end of the aisle. Usually she was bawling at me by now. Her bag was heavy and full of the night's milk and she was uncomfortable—but this morning she was silent.

"That horse scares you, doesn't he?" I murmured, pouring corn into her trough. "He won't hurt you. You scare him, too, I think. We all do." Betsy ignored me and thrust her head in. A second later, a crunching sound and the sweet smell of cracked corn filled the air. I set the pail in place and reached for the one-legged stool and the udder rag.

I settled myself on the stool, making sure of my balance before I leaned down and wiped the flecks of dung and hay off Betsy's udder. The rag was damp and cold, and she hunched her back.

I was a fast milker. It has to do with how strong your hands are, I think. That's what my pa used to say anyway. His hands were long-fingered and slender, but strong. So are mine.

I kept glancing behind myself at the stallion. He was watching me and Betsy intently. I sang my usual little tune to Betsy, using the squirts of milk hitting the pail as the rhythm. It was an Irish song, from my mother and grandmother. They sang it fast, like a jig; I liked to slow it down a little, drawing out the words. I had no idea what they meant. *Gaelic*, my mother called the language. She didn't speak it either. I wondered if we said the words right or if we were like Mr. Svensen, our old neighbor, getting everything backward and making funny mistakes, like asking if the plate was locket.

"Gate," my mother had corrected him in her gentlest voice. "And you mean *locked*, not *locket*."

I closed my eyes and sang a little louder, and I could see my mother's face. Betsy's flank was warm and soft. She was chewing happily, and I knew she liked my singing.

I sat up straight and turned to look back down the barn aisle again. The Mustang had lowered his head, and he blew a long breath out his nostrils when he saw me looking at him. "It's a song older than the stones, my mother always said," I told him.

I was careful to strip out the last drops of milk so that Betsy would keep producing—and to get every bit of the cream. Mrs. Stevens saved it up. She would have me churning butter in a day or two.

On the way past the stallion, I was careful to walk slowly, not to make any sudden motion. He watched me carefully. I could see that his water bucket was still upright. Good. I set the milk bucket down to put a little dried hay grass in his manger, then a coffee tin full of oats. Then I backed away.

"Hiram will feed you more later when he is done with his morning chores. Or maybe they will let you out to the pasture today and..."

I trailed off. I knew it wasn't true. Of course he wouldn't be let out into the pasture. Mr. Stevens was afraid to even try to get a halter on him, and Hiram wasn't being paid to break wild horses.

I swung around and picked up the milk bucket with one hand and lifted the lantern down with the other. I left quietly, trying not to scare the Mustang again. I was almost to the front door when I heard the whicker this time.

I turned. "I'll be back as soon as I can," I whispered. The stallion needed a friend. And I suppose I did, too.

CHAPTER FOUR

❧ ❧ ❧

*The little one comes every morning. She is gentle
and mild. I think she would let me go back out into the
sunshine if she could. I don't know where their lead mare
is, but the older male who comes sometimes is cruel.
Perhaps he has driven away most of his herd.*

*M*onday morning I woke long before dawn
and lay in my pantry, unhappy, thinking
about spring cleaning. Mrs. Stevens never missed
a day of housework. Her round of chores rolled
along like a cart wheel on a hard-packed road. Like
most women, she arranged her work according to
the days. I lay still, listing them in my mind, dread-
ing the extra work that would be added this week.

Monday was always wash day, and doing the laundry was the hardest, meanest, worst backbreaking
work we did—so we did it while we were still rested

from Sunday's Bible reading and rest—and a big Sunday supper. Every Monday I smelled lye soap from the neighboring farms and knew women were boiling laundry pots. I saw the tiny white rectangles of their bedding hanging from lines all down the valley.

If I squinted, and if it wasn't hot enough to make the air squirm and shimmer, I imagined that I could see far enough to see my father's farm, linens hung out on the clotheslines running between the three old cottonwood trees behind the house.

Tuesday we did the ironing since the laundry was still damp. Mrs. Stevens had a good set of irons. When I first came, it was my job to switch them out, placing the spare back on the woodstove, keeping the fire up to reheat them. Now she had me press pillowcases and tea cloths and the tablecloths she used every day.

Wednesday was sewing day since we had just been through all the clothes-washing and ironing. She always noticed tiny tears and little snags. It was my job to check buttons and stitch them down tight before they came off. She got upset if she found one missing—that meant I had missed a loose one. Mrs.

Stevens didn't really trust me to do anything else with a needle. My stitches weren't very even, which pained her more than it did me.

Thursday was market day. Usually it was Mr. Stevens who went. Mrs. Stevens spent time the night before making out her list of needful things. Sometimes she went with him. When she did, Thursday was like a second Sabbath for me. Even though she left me chores to do, I could do them at my own pace, and I could pretend it was my house, that I could decide what was for supper and tell people to mind their manners.

My first year at the Stevenses, I would pretend that Betsy, the horses, the dogs, and the chickens were all my friends, that I was having a party. Then it started to feel too silly doing it, and I stopped. I didn't have any friends anymore.

Friday was cleaning day. Mrs. Stevens focused her attention on a different room each week, and we'd move furniture to sweep beneath or mop the floors with extra care to get all the corners. She'd had me carrying fifty-pound mop buckets the day after Mr. Stevens brought me home to her. It had taken both hands, the bucket banging my shins at every step.

Saturday was baking day. I had loved Saturdays in my own home. My mother made bread, but she also made cakes and pies and cobblers, using fruit in the summer and squash in the winter. Mrs. Stevens made heavy, dark breads that tasted strongly of molasses and salt. Once in a long while she made a cobbler or a cake for a funeral—but I rarely got a taste. She thought sugar was too expensive to waste on me.

Sunday was always the day of rest. Mr. Stevens was very strict about the Sabbath. My parents hadn't worked on Sundays, either, but we had sung together, and sometimes we would all take a walk along the creek. Mama had always made a nice dinner if there was plenty of food, and Pa would let us play chess or checkers.

Mr. Stevens read the Bible aloud while his wife and I sat with our hands in our laps, listening. It could go on for a hours, some Sundays. I had learned not to fidget, but it was worse than church, by far—and Mr. Stevens wasn't interesting like Pa had always been. He didn't explain the scripture, and he didn't read it like a story, pouncing on some words and letting other trickle out slowly. His voice was loud and precise and flat—and endless.

The boss rooster crowed out in the coop, interrupting my sleepy thoughts. Mrs. Stevens was always about ten minutes behind the first rooster. I lit a candle and was up and dressed by the time she tapped on the pantry door.

"You're growing," she said, leading the way back up the hall. "Now you can be of some real use to me at housework."

I sighed. All I ever *did* was help her with her work.

"Do you have something to say to me, Miss Katie?"

I shook my head.

"That's good," she told me. "Rude children don't get letters."

I turned to face her squarely, my heart pounding. Had my uncle Jack written me at last? She waggled a finger in my face.

"Maybe that's why he hasn't answered." She smiled as though it was a joke between us. "Maybe he knows you are a rude girl that he wouldn't want to have in his home."

I exhaled slowly, fighting the ache behind my

eyes. When I had first come, Mrs. Stevens would hold me tightly when I cried, rocking me back and forth, calling me an orphan, a poor child. But she had lost patience quickly. Now she only got annoyed if she noticed tears in my eyes.

"Well," she said after a moment, straightening her apron. "We might as well get started."

I nodded.

She reached out and tapped the top of my head. "Go milk. I'll get the laundry water boiling. This afternoon we'll start in scrubbing the larder shelves."

I waited for her to turn away. Then I washed up and got a clean pail off the sideboard. My jacket was hanging beside the door. On my way out to the barn, Tiger came bounding up behind me, purring, braiding her steps with mine so that I nearly tripped over her. I shooed her back toward the house.

"You'll scare the Mustang if you're silly like this, chasing around the barn," I scolded her.

She arched her back and meowed, staring at the milk bucket.

"I'll make sure you get your milk," I promised. "Scat!" I rattled the bucket and chased her a few steps, then started back up the hill. It was only then that I noticed the barn door was already open. I could see lantern light through the doorway. I ran the rest of the way.

Mr. Stevens and a man I didn't know were standing in front of the Mustang's stall. He was as far away from them as he could get, switching his tail back and forth, nostrils flared.

"I'm not sure what to do, Mr. Harris," Mr. Stevens was saying.

The man glanced at me as I set down the bucket. "Morning, young lady."

I nodded politely and reached for the door handle. "You can leave it open, Katie," Mr. Stevens said.

I hesitated. He was still looking at me, so I spoke up. "Tiger is full of vinegar this morning, and she'll scare him." I gestured toward the Mustang.

Mr. Stevens shook his head. "*Everything* spooks him. Leave the door open."

I nodded and went to Betsy's stall. Maybe, if I hurried, I could meet Tiger on the path, and the prospect of warm milk would lure her back down to the house. I gave Betsy her corn and got to work. The milk smelled sweet; the morning was chilly enough that it steamed in the bucket.

I was nearly finished when I heard the stallion squeal. I stood up, expecting to see Tiger in the barn, drinking from his bucket. But that wasn't it at all. Mr. Harris had gone into his stall.

"Be careful of him," Mr. Stevens warned.

Mr. Harris nodded. "I will." He took a half step forward. "I just want to see how—"

He didn't finish his sentence because the Mustang reared, striking out. Mr. Harris stumbled backward, feeling behind himself for the gate latch. A second later, he was out of the stall, raking his hand through his hair, laughing nervously.

"See what I mean?" Mr. Stevens said as the stallion whirled in a circle, then kicked at the side of the stall. The crash of his hooves made me flinch. Betsy shifted. I rebalanced the one-legged stool and finished milking.

When I carried the full milk bucket past the stalls, Mr. Stevens and Mr. Harris were still standing there, hands on their hips, looking at the stallion. "I have no idea what do with him," Mr. Stevens was saying.

"I know a man who might could help." I heard Mr. Harris's answer just as I went out the door. "A Mr. Barrett. He's a good hand with horses."

Mr. Harris's voice faded as I started back to the house. I intercepted Tiger, on her way back up the hill. She smelled the milk and made a quick turn to follow me. I poured her saucer full before I went in.

"Is that you, Katie?" Mrs. Stevens shouted from the kitchen when she heard the back door open.

"Yes, ma'am," I called back.

"Come give me a hand with the wash water!"

I sighed. Her voice was shrill. I was pretty sure I hadn't done anything to upset her. Mr. Stevens might have been mean to her—or maybe she was upset because she had to start spring cleaning early because his cousin was coming to visit. I sighed. It didn't matter what she was upset about. She would end up scolding *me*.

CHAPTER FIVE

🙲 🙲 🙲

*It was odd how much I hoped to hear the footfalls of
the little one with the long mane. I also longed for the sky,
to be outside this strange den. I watched the other horses—
draped with metal and ropes—as they walked out into
the sunlight, and wished I could gallop past them, then
run on, away from the sunrise, toward my home.*

*T*he spring cleaning was even worse than
usual. The first day, we scrubbed the grease
out of every part of the kitchen. For a year,
meat drippings had spattered the hearthstones,
the floor planks, and the wall beside the woodstove.

By the third day, I was too tired to eat much
supper. Mrs. Stevens looked at me across the table.
"Maybe you should go on to bed now."

I looked outside. It was barely dark.

Mr. Stevens cleared his throat. His wife turned

to look at him. "I might hire someone to break the horse."

Mrs. Stevens made a little clucking sound. "Are you sure it wouldn't be better just to sell him?"

"To who?" Mr. Stevens exploded. "Who's going to buy a wild stallion that can't be used as a saddle horse or a plow horse?"

Mrs. Stevens ducked her head, and I knew what she was thinking. I was thinking the same thing. Mr. Stevens had been foolish enough to buy him. I covered my mouth with my napkin.

"It's some kind of weed they feed the Mustangs," he added. "It makes them feel sick without killing them, so they are calm for a day or two—long enough for the horse trader to leave town."

"That makes sense," Mrs. Stevens agreed instantly. "He certainly looked tame that first morning."

I thought about it. The Mustang had seemed more than tame. He had nearly stumbled going into the barn. If he had been rearing and fighting the rope, no one would have bought him.

"Liars and cheats are everywhere these days," Mr. Stevens said. "I've been thinking about going west."

Mrs. Stevens took in a breath so sharp that she coughed.

Mr. Stevens laughed quietly. "Calm down, wife. I met a man named Barrett. He's the one who knew about the stinkweed. He's here in Scott County talking to some of the neighbors about putting to-gether a wagon party to travel with him. Mr. Harris is considering it. You'd be surprised how many are thinking about going."

Mrs. Stevens glanced around the room, her gaze snagging on the newly scrubbed sideboard, hearth, floor planks, the walls we had washed that morning with scalding water and lye soap. Then she turned toward the little sitting room, and I saw her staring at her grandmother's red rugs.

"Martha!" Mr. Stevens said firmly. "If anything comes of the idea, I'll tell you. You know I won't do it unless I'm convinced it's the right thing. It's getting late this year anyway. Next spring would be soon enough."

Mrs. Stevens looked pale. "I can only hope you will consider my feelings in this matter."

Mr. Stevens smiled and nodded, then answered as though he hadn't heard her at all. "Barrett says the Oregon country is full of deer and elk and other game," he said. "There's tall timber and farm soil so rich the crops jump up out of the ground."

"Katie!" Mrs. Stevens snapped at me.

I jumped, startled.

She glared. "Why are you still here? I told you to get to bed!"

I stood up, barely hearing her angry voice and barely feeling my feet touch the floor. West! I wanted with all my heart to go west. I could find my uncle, and I knew he would take me in. He was my mother's brother, after all. I nearly danced my way down the hall, tired as I was. A year. It would go by slowly, but it would go by. In a year, surely I would get a letter from my uncle. I would know where he lived.

I dreamed that night of forests and mountains and a blue ocean and a family who met me at the door of a neat little farmhouse and pulled me inside, laughing and smiling and glad to see me. I couldn't really remember my uncle Jack's face, but in the dream he was tall and handsome, and his daughters were nice and called me their new sister.

When I woke up, it took a few minutes for me

to remember where I was. I sat up in the pantry and rubbed my eyes. The roosters were just starting to crow. I sighed and rose to dress.

"Tiger followed me this morning," I explained to the stallion the next day. It was chilly enough that my breath showed, hanging in the air. The instant I got the last word out, Tiger shot past me into the barn.

The stallion startled, tossing his head as she ran past. I heard a rustling in the spilled straw and knew she had found a mouse.

The Mustang pranced sideways in his stall, snapping his hooves up high, but he didn't look scared—he just looked like a horse that wants to have a good gallop. I took down the bucket and walked to the last stall, stopping to pat Delia and Midnight on the way. Mr. Stevens wasn't off as early as usual, so the buggy team was still warm and sleepy in their stalls. The plow team was out to pasture—Hiram was working up the valley somewhere for a few days.

I rubbed the mares' foreheads and told them I had missed them, with Mr. Stevens gone so early every morning. They both nuzzled my neck and breathed their warm grassy breath down my collar.

I glanced back and saw the Mustang watching me.

Betsy was glad to see me, too, in her way. She bawled once, to let me know she hadn't appreciated my taking time to talk to the horses. As I milked her, she chewed her corn and batted her thick lashes when she lifted her head to look at me. I milked her as fast as I could, then put away the stool. Through the open door, the sky was getting lighter, turning pinkish in the east. It was chilly, but the sharp winter bite had gone out of the cold.

"The Stevenses might go west," I told the stallion. I shivered and pulled my jacket closer. "That'd mean I could find my uncle Jack."

Tiger was back out in the barn aisle now, toying with the mouse she had caught. The Mustang watched her closely, looking back and forth between us. I set the milk bucket down.

"Did you come from the west somewhere?" I asked him. He tossed his mane and sidled uneasily back from the gate when I took a step forward. "Tell me," I said in a gentle voice. "What's it like?"

Tiger came to rub against my legs.

The stallion backed away.

"She can't hurt you," I told him. "Look." I bent

to pick Tiger up, getting a tight hold on her legs.

The stallion snorted and danced sideways.

"Just come closer, and you'll see she's harmless," I pleaded with him. "If you don't settle down, Mr. Stevens is going to hire someone to teach you what for. Maybe, anyway..." I added, just to be honest with him. "He doesn't like spending money if he doesn't have to."

Tiger squirmed in my arms, and I scratched her behind her ears. She relaxed almost immediately, closing her eyes. The stallion turned his head, watching closely.

"See?" I reassured him. "Look at that. She's gentle. She isn't even that good a mouser." The stallion took one step toward me, then stood like a statue for a long moment. Then he came forward again. I held Tiger still as he put his head over the stall. I held my breath as he sniffed at Tiger, then scented my hair, my cheek. The stallion tossed his head, then touched my cheek once more, his breath warm on my ear.

My heart was pounding as he moved toward the back of his stall again and stood watching me as I let Tiger jump to the ground. He was beginning to trust me! "Thank you," I breathed as I backed away. No horse had ever seemed so powerful to me, so dangerous, and yet he had touched my face as gently as a friend would have.

"I have to go or Mrs. Stevens will come looking for me," I told him. "We empty the mattresses today and refill with them with the corn husks we dried last fall." The stallion looked at me, his head high, his neck arched.

"Then I have to wash the windows," I said. "It'll be warm enough by midday to do that."

I sighed, wondering what anyone would think if they heard me talking like this to a wild horse. "It's market day, so at least Mr. Stevens will be gone most the afternoon. I hope so anyway."

"Katie?"

"That's Mrs. Stevens, wondering what's taking so long," I told him, backing away. I blew out the lantern and hung it up, then came back for the milk bucket. Tiger smelled the warm milk and trailed along behind me as I went down the path toward the house. That night, lying on my pallet, I thought about the Mustang. If I was careful not to startle him again, he would trust me more and more each day. I went to sleep and dreamed of tall forests and the Mustang running through the trees.

The next morning, I milked Betsy so fast even she looked surprised. I heard the rooster crowing down in the coop as I stood and talked to the stallion again. This time, he stayed at the back of his stall until I picked up the bucket to leave. I was almost at the door when I heard him snort and paw the ground. I glanced back. He was at the front of the stall, reaching out, stretching his neck, looking right at me.

I hung the bucket from a branch on the ash tree just outside the barn door, then went back in. The stallion was still reaching over the stall gate.

"You're not skinny anymore," I told him. "I think you're beautiful."

He tossed his head and pawed at the dirt.

I took another step forward.

He shook his mane again, and I could see how matted it was. A currycomb might not be enough. It might have to be cut off. "It's all right," I whispered. "I would never hurt you." I reached out slowly, keeping my hand steady. I touched his cheek, for a long moment. Then I ran my hand down his neck to his shoulder. He let me do it twice more, then whirled and went to stand by the back wall.

I stood looking at him, astonished. He had trusted me to touch him. My thoughts were interrupted by a sudden warm pressure against my leg. Before I could stop her, Tiger slipped between the stall rails and put her front paws up the edge of his water bucket.

I watched the stallion come forward, his head lowered, his ears flickering from back to front, curious, but ready to fight if he had to.

"Tiger? Kitty, kitty, come back," I pleaded, but she was too busy lapping up the cool water to care if some silly horse came close to her.

"Katieeee!"

It was Mrs. Stevens, shouting from the porch. Any other day I would have shouted back to tell her I was coming, but I didn't want to shout. Not now. The stallion took a step forward, then stopped, stretching out his long neck, his nostrils wide. His muzzle was within a few inches of the cat. She seemed not to notice him at all.

Tiger finished drinking and went back on all fours, graceful and silent as any cat. She came out between the rails and rubbed herself on my leg, purring. "Good for you!" I told the stallion.

The Mustang stamped one hind leg. It was too early for flies to be tickling him. His eyes were so intense. It really seemed as though he was trying to tell me something.

"You could squash her with one hoof," I guessed. "Yes, you could. Why were you ever scared of something so small?"

"Katieeee!"

I wanted, more than anything, to stay right where I was, to talk to the Mustang until he let me touch him again.

"Katieeee!" Mrs. Stevens sounded pretty angry. If she had to come up the hill to get an answer from me... "I better go," I told the stallion. I stepped back. "I'll come back tonight or before. Whatever happens, I'll come as soon as I can."

The Mustang looked at me so intently, it was as though he was about to say something, about to speak. I tiptoed out, careful to move slowly until I got outside. Then I lifted the bucket down from the branch and walked as fast as I could toward the house.

When I was halfway down the path, the boss rooster crowed, loud and long. An instant later, the top of the sun rose above the horizon. Streaks of gold light shot across the valley. The cedar trees by the river looked nearly black. It was so beautiful, I caught my breath. Then I noticed a horse tied to the hitching rail—a tall red roan. I had never seen it before. I slowed my step and veered to go in the back door.

CHAPTER SIX

※ ※ ※

*There is a sage smell in the wind sometimes.
It's faint and weak, as though it has traveled many
days to reach me. I welcome it. So few scents
make it into the wooden box where I am trapped.
I am starved for scents, for living air.*

"Katie?" Mrs. Stevens called the instant she
heard the door close.

"Yes, ma'am," I answered her. "Just now cooling
the milk."

"You're slow as winter molasses this morning,"
she said, standing at the head of the hallway, scolding me gently. "Wash up. We have company."

I wanted to ask her who it was, but she turned
and walked back into the parlor. Who would be
visiting so early in the morning? I got the milk
cooling, leaving just enough in the bucket to fill

Tiger's saucer on the porch. Then I washed the bucket carefully, going as fast as I could. I took a second to smooth my hair a little and rinsed my hands and face in the washbasin. I went down the hall, hoping whichever neighbor it was would leave soon. I wanted to get enough work done so that I'd have a little extra time to steal away if I could. The Mustang trusted me a little more every time I talked to him.

I wished it weren't spring cleaning week. It was always hard for me to slip away to the barn. It would be nearly impossible to sneak out there until all the extra work was finished.

My thoughts were stilled the instant I came around the corner. There was a man sitting at the table with Mr. Stevens. He wore a hat so broad-brimmed that it nearly hid his face. It was strange that he would wear it indoors at all. Even in the early morning light, even with the wide brim overhanging his face, I could tell his skin was browned the color of coffee from the sun. He wasn't any neighbor I had ever met.

"There you are!" Mrs. Stevens exclaimed. Her hands were fluttering from her face to her bodice, then back. "Run and bring in the eggs," she said, and her hands swooped together to shoo me toward the door. I got the egg basket off the sideboard and went out.

We hadn't gathered eggs the day before—too much work in the house. So, even though the hens were still sleepy and grumpy, I found fourteen eggs. Mrs. Stevens was still fussing when I went back in. She had boiled coffee and was pouring it.

She hovered over the egg basket like it was something she had never seen before in her life. I had never seen her so nervous. Maybe the man was from the bank? My mother had gotten like that when the bankers had paid a call.

"Sit," Mrs. Stevens said, shooing me again. "Eat."

There was a bowl of plain oatmeal on the table. Mine. I sidled toward it. The men were talking in low voices about oxen. Maybe Mr. Stevens was buying a team of oxen to plow? Some men swore they were better than horses for that kind of slow, steady work.

I slid into my chair and tried to be invisible. My bowl of oats wasn't steaming. I picked up my spoon and tasted them. Cold. I looked up, meaning to ask someone to pass the honey, but the men were lost in their conversation, and Mrs. Stevens was walking back to the woodstove.

"The eggs will only take a few minutes," Mrs. Stevens said from the stove.

Mr. Stevens waved one hand at her to let her know he had heard.

"It takes—" Mr. Stevens began.

"Five months. Sometimes six," the man interrupted. "I will leave early, as early as the weather will let me."

Mr. Stevens nodded. "And land out there is—"

"Free or cheap," the man interrupted him again. "The best plots are going fast. Waiting a year can be a mistake."

In that instant, I finally understood what was going on, and my stomach tightened. This man didn't look like a farmer because he wasn't one. His hat was odd because it was the kind of hat a man could wear in every kind of weather. This man had something to do with going west. And Mr. Stevens was thinking about going *this* year?

Mr. Stevens kept asking questions. I ate my oats, then sat as still as a stone, listening to them. Mrs. Stevens had heated a skillet; I could hear the eggs snapping and sizzling in the pork fat, the scrape of the fork as she stirred them.

My heart was pounding. If we were really going, I could write my uncle Jack again and just tell him I was coming. It would be all right, I was sure. It had to be.

Mrs. Stevens cleared her throat, and I glanced up. She was bringing plates of steaming scrambled eggs and slab ham to set in front of the men.

"The chance for new-opened land is hard to pass up," the man was saying. "Only fools sit and watch the opportunity of a generation go past them. And you don't look like a fool to me, sir."

Mr. Stevens squared his shoulders and sat up straighter in his chair. "I'm not known for foolishness," he said.

"Many sensible men have decided not to go, haven't they, Mr. Barrett?" Mrs. Stevens said quietly as she straightened up. "My husband hasn't settled on anything yet."

The man turned to look at her. "Your husband sounds pretty interested to me," he said, grinning. He touched his hat respectfully. "Don't worry, ma'am. Most farm women get used to the wagon life fairly quickly. You'll see."

I lowered my head and picked up my spoon,

intent on being invisible long enough to hear all I could from Mr. Barrett before Mrs. Stevens sent me back to my chores. It didn't work. She noticed me less than a minute later.

"Katie?"

I glanced at her. She was wiping her hands on her apron, her face stern and hard.

"Yes, ma'am?"

"Start with those mattresses now."

I sighed and got up. The corn shucks were in the woodshed. I bagged what we would need for the Stevenses' bed and carried them in the back door. By then, Mr. Barrett was leaving. Whatever else they said, I had missed.

🐚 🐚 🐚

The spring cleaning dragged itself along—finally it was finished—at the end of *two* weeks, not one. And then it was March. It didn't *feel* like spring. It got colder than it had been all winter.

We had a snowstorm, and Hiram left off flattening the cornstalks from the year before to go help Mr. Firner slaughter his pigs for the year. The cold weather kept the meat fresher until they could get it into the smokehouse and packed in salt.

It got so cold that Mr. Stevens moved Midnight and Delia and the plow team back into the barn day and night. I had to fill the chicken coop in deep straw to keep the one batch of early-hatch chicks alive. Tiger moved back into the barn, too, and insisted on getting her milk there. She refused to walk a snowy path if she didn't have to. It was all right. The Mustang knew she was harmless now.

The Mustang seemed to like having horse company all the time. From the first night that all the other stalls were full, he seemed calmer and more content. He always watched when I scratched Midnight's ears and combed out Delia's mane and tail.

If I had time to stand still in front of his stall and talk quietly to him for a while, he would usually come to the gate and let me touch him—but only if I was the only one in the barn. If Hiram or Mr. Stevens came in, he stood at the back of the stall again.

Hiram was always patient and quiet-voiced. The stallion watched closely when he came in every morning to clean the stalls and feed. Hiram always talked to him, too, but the Mustang never came to the front of the stall for Hiram.

I could tell that Hiram was uneasy sitting around the Stevenses' house. When the snow eased up, he would be glad to go back to clearing last year's cornstalks in the two fields where Mr. Stevens had left them standing last fall.

The ears in those two fields had been too small to harvest before first frost because Mr. Stevens had planted late. He had brought in half a crop, at best.

Every morning, I stood in front of the Mustang's stall before I milked Betsy. "Will you let me touch you today?" I asked him.

He always reacted. Sometimes he would switch his tail back and forth; sometimes he would blow out a long breath. But it seemed like he could understand me.

"The ground is still frozen," I said to him one day. "But as soon as it thaws for good, Mr. Stevens will put the other horses out in the pasture. Don't you want to go out, too?"

He was standing at the back of his stall, looking at me. He stamped a forehoof and walked forward, stopping so that his muzzle was directly above the stall gate. I took a single step toward him, then stopped. I stood still for a moment, then I stepped forward again—a slow half step, and I kept my arms close to my body. He was still wary of me, of any human being.

I came forward, raising my hand slowly, and held it open, palm up, just in front of him. He whuffled a breath out through his nostrils. Then there was a prickly tickle of his whiskers, a warm sigh— and the smell of sweet grass from his breath. I patted his cheek, then let my hand slide down his neck. He smelled my hair, my cheek, then my hand again. Then, without warning, he shied away from me, spinning in a circle, his hooves throwing clods of dirt against the planks.

I heard a low-pitched chuckle, and I turned toward the door. Mr. Stevens was standing there. "That's good," he said. "Maybe if you get him gentled a little, I can get him trained."

I managed to nod, but the idea of Mr. Stevens training the Mustang made me cringe. He was awkward in the saddle, and he always carried a whip and jerked the reins when he drove the buggy. I pitied the mares.

"You've been hearing all the talk about going west," he said.

I nodded, keeping my face expressionless. He had never talked to me beyond giving me scoldings or reminding me to finish some chore.

"You can tell that Mrs. Stevens doesn't want to go?"

I nodded again, cautiously. Anyone could tell. Whenever he brought it up at the table, she looked ill with worry.

He sighed. "Has she said much about it to you?"

I shook my head. "Nothing at all, sir."

He looked down at the toe of his work boot, then back at me. I was afraid he might come closer and scare the Mustang again. But he only shook his head; then, without another word to me, he turned and walked away. From halfway down the path, I heard him shouting. Mrs. Stevens answered from inside the house.

"I'll be done with Betsy in a few minutes," I whispered to the Mustang. He flared his nostrils. Now he looked fierce again, and wild. But when he had touched me, he had been so careful, so gentle.

I wished with all my heart that Mr. Stevens had not chosen that moment to come into the barn. Maybe the Mustang would never come close to me again.

By the time I was finished milking, the stallion had come to the front of his stall once more. But when he saw me walking toward him, he backed away.

"That's all right," I told him as I came closer. "I understand. I talk to someone and then I get shy again, too."

"Katieeeeee!"

Mrs. Stevens was shouting from the house, and I felt anger rise in my heart like a flock of startled crows. I stopped and set down the heavy bucket. I wanted to scream at her to leave me alone, just for once, just for a little while. But I knew it would do no good to make her angry with me.

I had learned that the first week I had lived here. Mrs. Stevens had made me stand in the corner nearly a full day, until I had apologized for saying her fried chicken was not as good as my own mother's. I had only been six, and it was true—and saying it had made me cry, missing Mama. But she punished me anyway.

"Kaaaatie!"

I clenched my fists and wondered what it would feel like not to have anyone shout at me for a whole day. My parents had been strict, but they had smiled and laughed a lot, too. My sister had been one of the silliest, cutest little girls; her giggles had made everyone else laugh....

Mrs. Stevens yelled again. I fumbled for the bucket bale and started to walk, my eyes stinging with tears. I heard a whicker, and I put out one hand to touch Midnight's forehead as I passed. But hot tears blurred my vision, and I doubled over.

My stomach muscles were jerking and my shoulders shook, and there was nothing I could do about any of it. I wanted my family. It could not be true that they were gone. It just could *not* have happened, not all of them, all at once.

The pain inside me swelled to fill my skin. I sobbed, setting down the bucket blindly, then backed away from it, barely feeling the stall rails against my back.

I braced myself, leaning hard, and the crying just took me over; I had no choice *but* to cry this time. I was so sad and so tired of living where no one loved me. They didn't even act like they liked me most of the time.

I covered my mouth with one shaky hand, afraid I would throw up. It felt more like I was vomiting than like I was crying—I had felt so bad for so long. I knew Mrs. Stevens was probably still shouting my name, but I couldn't hear her. I couldn't hear anything but the ragged little sounds coming out of my own mouth. The stall rails dug into my back, and it hurt. It hurt to cry. *Everything* hurt.

A light, warm touch on my shoulder made me turn, eyes still closed. Poor Midnight, I thought, I had scared her. She was warm and calm as always, and I reached up to hug her, leaning on her, crying against her neck, grateful that at least the animals here were my friends.

Then my fingers crossed a matted clump of mane, and my heart skipped a beat. I knew I should step back, that if I scared the Mustang, he might rear and hurt me. But I couldn't stop crying, and the Mustang stood with me another full minute, until I had fought the sobs to a standstill. Then I felt him lift his head as he drew back.

I released my hold on his neck instantly, opening my eyes. I knew he didn't want to be leaned on, clutched at. He had done it for me.

"What in the world are you doing up there, Katie?"

Mrs. Stevens was really shouting now; her harsh voice made me pull in a quick breath. Was she coming up the path? She sounded closer, but I couldn't tell *how* close. I wiped at my face with my dress sleeve, trying to think.

The milk bucket was upright. There were no bits of straw floating in it. I wouldn't be in trouble if I hurried. I picked up the bucket and then turned back to the Mustang.

"Thank you," I whispered. The words weren't nearly enough, and I knew it. But I meant them with all my heart.

CHAPTER SEVEN

✿ ✿ ✿

The little one was so frightened, so sad.
I was careful not to hurt her. The sage scent came
again after she had gone, fainter this time. I had
to lift my head and breathe deep. I want to follow it,
chase it through the wind all the way home.

*M*r. Barrett came back to the house twice in the next two weeks. Hiram sat and listened the second time—and two neighbors showed up, as well. Mr. Themble and Mr. Dulin sat with their jaws set hard, taking in every word.

Mr. Barrett spent a long time talking about what people ought to take, what they ought to leave behind. Then Mr. Stevens asked questions about the provisions, the grass along the trails, the lay of the land in Oregon.

I listened intently. Mr. Themble wanted to know

about cattle ranching more than farming. Mr. Dulin asked twice about the timber, if there were sawmills or at least deep enough rivers to run the water-wheels so they could be built if a man cared to invest his time and effort.

"You have good maps?" Hiram asked quietly. That brought them back around to talking about the route, the journey, the hardships of the trail.

Through all this, I sat near the kitchen stove on the floor, silent as a mouse, barely moving. The men finally talked themselves to a standstill, and there was a half minute of silence.

"How are farmers doing who have been out west a few years?" Mrs. Stevens asked. All the men turned to look at her. I was sure they had forgotten she was there, just as they had forgotten me. She had to know that Mr. Stevens would be upset with her for interrupting the men. Her voice was shaking a little. So were her hands.

Mr. Stevens looked stunned when she pulled out a chair and sat at the table across from Mr. Barrett.

He smiled uneasily. "They do well enough, by all accounts."

Mrs. Stevens pulled in a breath. "That's what they say when you ask them?"

He shrugged. "Not directly."

She waited, studying his face. Mr. Stevens looked as though someone had punched him in the stomach. I had never once seen Mrs. Stevens defy his wishes like this. His face was dark as a storm sky. Her hands were knotted in her lap.

Mr. Barrett readjusted his hat. "I've guided two parties west, ma'am. One to Oregon and one to California."

Mrs. Stevens looked ill. "Only two? So you haven't been back to either place to ask how people do?"

He smiled. "The settlements are growing like weeds, ma'am."

She cleared her throat. "Davenport has had a courthouse for six years now. We have bakeries, a forge, a dry goods store. Is the land so much better out west?"

Mr. Barrett smiled again, his easy, wide smile. "More go every year, ma'am, so it must be as good as they say. A few come back, but—"

"Why?" Mrs. Stevens's eyes were hard as stone. "Why would they—"

Mr. Stevens slapped the table, open-handed, cutting her off. "I apologize for my wife, sir," he said, then turned to look at her. "Hush, Martha. Not another word."

Mrs. Stevens sat stock-still. She stared at the tabletop, her face perfectly blank as the silence swelled up and filled the room, pressing against the walls.

"There's no fever or other sickness in Oregon, is there?" Hiram asked after an awkward minute had ticked past. I looked past Mrs. Stevens at Mr. Barrett.

"No," he said. "No cholera, no cankers, nothing to speak of. There are no swamps or marshes, and the air isn't heavy."

Mrs. Stevens stood abruptly, excusing herself. She boiled more coffee for the men, standing near the stove, her back toward them.

I moved out of her way, finding another spot on the floor—a much chillier one, but I didn't want to go to bed until I had to.

After the men left and Mr. Stevens came back in from walking them out, he told her it was time to retire for the night. She made her shooing motion at me. I went down the hall without complaint, grateful she hadn't noticed me sooner.

I could hear Mr. Stevens scolding her, his voice tight and angry. Later, the sound of her weeping in the parlor was the only sound in the house. I am not sure when she went back to bed. Finally, I fell asleep.

Mr. Barrett came three more times. Mrs. Stevens made supper, and he ate with relish, complimenting the food. She nodded politely and said no more than she had to.

I listened as long as I was allowed, each time. Once I had to go to bed, I left the pantry door open a crack so that I could still hear bits and pieces of what they were saying as I fell asleep. Some of it scared me. But I still longed to go.

As the days passed, the weather turned milder, but the snow stuck and the path to the barn was slippery when I went out to the barn. On the mornings after Mr. Barrett's visits, I told the Mustang what I had heard. He stood close, sniffing at my hair and hands, his eyes wide and alert. Sometimes I thought he almost understood me. I wished that he could talk. He probably knew the country out west better than Mr. Barrett ever would.

Hiram was gone most the time now. He was shoveling hard snow off walks and roofs on what he called the widow farms. The fever had taken a lot of grown men along with my pa.

I knew it wouldn't be too much longer before the weather softened. I wondered how many would be on their way west instead of plowing this year. I hoped we would.

"There's a quilting party next Friday," Mr. Stevens announced one morning at breakfast. He smiled broadly at his wife, then at me.

I couldn't help but stare at him. Since when had he cared about quilting parties or anything the women of Scott County did together?

Mrs. Stevens tipped her head to one side. "Yes, I know. Violet Dulin stopped by the other day. I was out clearing off the garden beds. I told her I wouldn't be coming."

"Why?" Mr. Stevens asked sharply.

"Your cousin should be here about then," Mrs. Stevens said mildly. "I thought it best if I stayed home and kept up my housework."

He frowned. "I think you should go."

Mrs. Stevens opened her mouth, then closed it

and nodded when his face hardened. That evening I saw her bring her patch bag out, and she began stitching squares together the moment supper was over. She would need something started so she could work on it while she chatted with the other women at the party.

My endless circle of chores went on. Betsy didn't care at all how fast I milked her or how little attention I paid to her afterward—not so long as she got her corn and hay. So I milked fast, then I talked to the Mustang. Delia and Midnight would sometimes whicker at me, and I could tell they were jealous.

Mr. Stevens still got up early and had Hiram hitch up the buggy team by lantern light. But he wasn't drinking coffee in other people's kitchens and talking about the weather all day now. He was off to talk to men who were going west. He came back with lists of supplies and drawings and maps. Mrs. Stevens was tight-lipped and quiet in the evening as he pored over his papers.

Since the morning I had cried, the Mustang had changed his opinion of me. "You've probably decided I'm just too pitiful to be dangerous," I told him one morning, dragging my fingers through his mane. I had gotten a lot of the tangles out. He still wouldn't tolerate a currycomb.

The stallion shook his mane, and the motion went down his whole body, like a shiver he couldn't control. He stamped one forehoof, then the other. Then he turned and walked around the stall, forced into a tight circle by the planks and rails.

He had been cooped up in the stall so long, it was making him nervous and restless. Sometimes his pacing upset Delia and Midnight. Once or twice even the staid old plow team had whinnied and pawed at the dirt floors of their stalls when he was circling his own, tossing his head and squealing and switching his tail.

"Take it easy," I whispered to him one morning. He stopped for me to rub his forehead, then walked another circle. It was awful to watch his pacing. It was a big stall, but the stallion hadn't been out of it once since he had been brought to the farm.

I knew why. Mr. Stevens was still afraid to try to lead him out to pasture. So was Hiram; he had admitted it. He had also patted the top of my head one day and told me I was doing the Mustang real good by calming him down. He said I had a way with horses and would make a good trainer. I had laughed and so had he. Girls weren't horse trainers.

"I wish Hiram were here," I told the stallion. "I could use his advice." I rubbed his forehead. He shook his mane and raised his head high. He had heard some little sound, a mouse in the straw, most likely. He heard things the other horses never noticed.

"The weather will soon be warmer," I told him. "Midnight and Delia will get put out in the pastures." I rubbed the stallion's ears, and he closed his eyes as I got the mosquito bites he couldn't reach by rubbing against the stall planks.

"Would you let me put a halter and lead rope on you?"

He tossed his head and then let me pat his neck for a moment before he turned and paced again.

"If you would, I could probably talk Mr. Stevens into letting you run in the pasture at least sometimes," I told him as he came back around.

I rubbed his forehead as he swayed back and forth. Then he paced the circle again. It hurt me to watch him; it was wrong to keep him penned in like this.

I ran to the barn door and looked back down the path to the house. Mrs. Stevens was out in the vegetable patch by the road. I was supposed to join her when I was done with milking and emptying the night buckets into the privy.

I stared at her, working the half-thawed ground. Would she notice if I took a few extra minutes? Even if she did, she would shout at me from the garden a few times before she walked up to the barn. I would have time to pretend I had been cleaning the tack room or something.

I hung the milk bucket in the ash tree to keep Tiger out of it, then ran into the tack room. It smelled of mice and leather grease. The pegs on the right-hand wall held the carriage harness and the heavy-strapped plow rig. The back wall had three saddle trees jutting out. Only one had a saddle on it—and it was seldom used. Mr. Stevens always took the buggy.

Above the saddle trees were two pegs. One held two bridles, the nickel-plated bits covered in dust. The other had five or six halters, all well used.

I looked through them quickly. Two were buckled at their last holes—made as big as they could be for the plow team. I finally settled on an old one, the leather worn soft. I carried it back out into the aisle.

The Mustang was watching me. I walked slowly,

letting him get a good look at the halter. He paced his circle three or four times, stopping long enough to stare, then letting his nervousness explode into a half minute of rearing and head tossing.

"I know you hate the idea," I said, sure it was true. After all, ropes and leather were the things that had gotten him here, caged in this stall. How could I get him to believe that a halter was the way out, too?

"Will you trust me enough to at least look at it?" I pleaded with him.

He was frantic now, switching his tail and breathing harder. "It won't hurt you," I promised.

I took one more step forward. Just then, Tiger came racing across the barn and pounced on the end of the lead rope. I turned to look at her and realized something. The long lead looked like a snake trailing through the straw behind me.

I pulled the leather strap away from Tiger and slowly coiled it up. Then I faced the Mustang again.

He was still agitated, but he had stopped switching his tail. I risked a half step, then another half step. When I was close enough to the rail for him to reach out and sniff at the halter, I waited.

He paced his circle three times, then stopped and leaned out over the rail. I held the halter still, letting him touch it and smell the leather for a long moment. I stood very still, letting him assure himself that the halter meant him no harm.

"Katie!"

I sighed. Mrs. Stevens had missed me. What a surprise. I sighed. "I have to go," I told the stallion. "I always have to go." I put the halter behind my back and reached out with my free hand. He let me pat him, and tug gently at his mane. I kissed his muzzle. The velvety hair tickled my lips and nose. Then I ran to hang the halter back up and hurried outside.

CHAPTER EIGHT

❧ ❧ ❧

The straps and ropes are in her hands now. I cannot think
that she would mean to hurt me, but then, what does
she want? Oh, how I long to beat down this box, to smash
it into pieces so that I can run beneath the wide sky again.

At first, I had been preoccupied with gen-
tling the Mustang to halter and lead rope
so he could get out of the dim and dusty barn. But
as the days passed and Mr. Stevens and the other
men were meeting nearly every night to talk, I knew
there was another, even more important reason.
If we were going to go west, he had to calm down
and let himself be led along without fighting the
halter. If he wouldn't, Mr. Stevens might decide
to sell him after all.

I started sneaking off to the barn every time I had

a chance. It didn't take too long before the Mustang was comfortable enough with the halter just to sniff it matter-of-factly when I showed it to him. And after he had reassured himself about the halter, he would nuzzle my shoulder, hoping to have his ears scratched. I did, rubbing the halter along the side of his face, sliding it across his muzzle.

One morning I slid the leather over his muzzle, and pushed the crown strap gently over his ears. He was startled and paced, but when nothing happened to hurt or scare him, he came back and let me rub his forehead.

Once he was used to the halter, I tried tugging gently on the straps. The first time, he plunged backward, startled and angry. I hung on for a second, and he nearly lifted me off me feet. My arm was strained—it was sore for days. I made sure Mrs. Stevens didn't notice.

I kept trying gentle tugs on the halter, but the stallion always reacted the same way. It worried me. Every time I tried to control his movements, even for a second, he was ready to fight. How could I ever get him to calm down? I was pretty sure I didn't have much longer.

The fields were about due to plow. Any other year, Mr. Stevens would have been cleaning and mending the harness, making sure the plow was sharp, laying out the year's crops, buying seed corn— but this year he wasn't doing any of it. He would have been worried about Hiram being so busy else- where, too, but this year he didn't seem to care at all.

One morning a man came and bought the plow team. I gave each of them a cube of sugar from the pantry and hugged them good-bye. Mrs. Stevens watched as the man led the heavy-boned draft horses away. She kept chewing at her lower lip, like a child about to cry.

That evening, Mr. Stevens came home with oxen— twelve of the heavy beasts. He put them in the pasture and faced his wife.

"If we decide not to go, they can pull the plow."

Mrs. Stevens's eyes were narrow. "Six plows, if need be," she said quietly, and turned on her heel. He glared at her as she walked away.

I stayed to myself as much as I could. I day- dreamed, pretending my uncle Jack's letter would come the day before we were to leave. He'd say he was so glad that I was coming. He would tell me about his lovely, kind wife. They would have five children. One or two of them would be girls about my age, and we would grow up together, like sisters.

I lay on my pallet listening to the men talking in the kitchen and wished I would be allowed to ask questions. I wanted to know about the schoolhouses out west. Were they small and cozy like the ones here, with all the students in one or two rooms? Did they have woodstoves against the winter chill? Uncle Jack would let me go to school, I was sure of that. He wouldn't make me work all the time like the Stevenses did. I fell asleep nearly every night thinking about the journey west.

One evening when the wind smelled like rain, Mr. Stevens sat reading a guidebook. I could see the cover. It had been written by a man named Lansford D. Hasting. I had seen other guidebooks. Medorem Crawford had written one, and a man named Asa Lovejoy. The men were passing them around, discussing what they read.

Mrs. Stevens was cutting quilt pieces from the cloth in her patch bag that evening again. She was working with blues and reds, cut like stars. It was windy outside, and the noise of the ash trees groaning as they swayed sounded odd and spooky.

I was shelling and picking walnuts, trying to get most of them out whole so Mrs. Stevens wouldn't scold me. She finally went to bed. Mr. Stevens nodded without looking up from the page when she bade him good night. I cleaned up the flecks of walnut shell and the paper-thin casings that had held the nut meats in place, then I excused myself, too. He acted as though he hadn't heard me.

I lay awake until I heard Mr. Stevens retire for the night, then I lit a candle stub and read my mother's book for a little while. When my eyelids felt heavy, I blew out the candle.

But the wind was rising, and I couldn't go to sleep, no matter how many times I turned over and readjusted the blankets. The night crept past, silent except for the sound of the wind rushing past, shoving at the walls.

After a long time I could hear the Mustang whinnying. Midnight and Delia were in the barn tonight; Hiram had put them in on the chance that it stormed. The stallion was usually calm enough if they were in, too.

I kept listening, hoping the Mustang would quiet down, but he didn't. It was odd. There was no lightning. It wasn't raining yet, and, even if it did, rainstorms hadn't scared him before this.

I turned over once more and closed my eyes firmly, but I could not seem to let my weariness carry me into sleep. I kept listening. The stallion was squealing, the high-pitched sound he made when he was terrified.

I got up and stood shivering for a moment in the dark. Then I pulled my clothes on. I would just settle him down a little, then come back to bed.

There were flickers of lightning on the horizon when I went out the back door, but it was far away. My hair whipping around my face, I ran up the hill to the barn and opened the door, fighting the wind to close it behind myself. Feeling my way in the dark, I lit the lantern wick and hung it on the wall hook by the tack room, then turned around. I stood still as a stone, blinking in the honey-colored light.

The stallion had broken the latch on the stall gate. It was dangling by one peg. He was out, standing proud at the end of the barn aisle, his nostrils flared. I bit my lip, frantically trying to figure out what to do. He reared, lashing out at empty air. He was free at last, and if the barn door had been open, I knew he would have run twenty miles before he stopped. I took a step toward him, wondering if he would hurt me now that there were no stall rails between us.

The sky outside the flashed blue-white. I saw the brilliant light for an instant through the missing chinks in the planked walls. The roll of thunder ended in a dull crackling.

The stallion squealed and whirled in a tight circle, half rearing as he shied. Then he came back to earth and launched himself into a gallop. I barely had time to jump out of his way.

The barn aisle was long and wide, but the stallion could only manage about five strides before he had to plunge, rearing, and sliding to a halt before the closed door. He reared, pivoting on his hind legs, and sprang into a gallop again. This time I stepped backward into the tack room and stood still, watching.

The Mustang ran the length of the aisle again, then reared, pivoted, and started back. He was beautiful, like a magical creature from a book. He lunged back into a gallop after every pivoting turn. All his pent-up energy was finally exploding.

I was so glad to have come, so glad to have lit the lantern for him. Now that the darkness was gone, he ran without fear. His hooves flinging dirt and straw, he galloped back and forth so many times that I lost count. His breath was coming in heaving sobs when he finally slowed, then broke back into a trot, still rearing at the end of the aisle and whirling around to trot back.

I was afraid of him like this. His neck was arched, and he was prancing. The lightning flashed, and he kicked high, his back hooves striking the wall higher than my head.

Finally he dropped back to a walk after what seemed like hours. I saw the uncontrollable fire in his eyes subside, his head dropping a little. I could tell when he remembered that I was there. He stopped and looked at me.

"You have to go back in the stall tonight," I said sadly. "But I'll make sure you get to run again; as many nights as I can sneak out, you'll get to run." I meant it as a solemn promise.

I carried hay to where he stood, then ran to get a handful of corn and his halter. He ate it while I slipped the leather over his head. When I tugged gently at the halter he followed me uncertainly. He balked at the stall gate. I talked quietly, promising him it wasn't permanent.

He walked in cautiously. I pulled the gate closed and used the lead rope to tie it shut. Then I slid the halter off and scratched his ears until he moved away from me to drink from his bucket. I fetched more hay.

Then my knees went rubbery. If I hadn't heard him, if Mr. Stevens had found him first and tried to force him into the stall with the whip...

I found a mallet and repegged the latch. It was bent, but I managed to make it work again. Mr. Stevens wouldn't notice. He almost never came to the barn now.

The Mustang lifted his head to watch as I used a hay rake to smooth out the worst of the hoof gouges in the aisle and scattered straw over the ground. I blew out the lantern and went out, wrestling with the wind for control of the door until I finally got the bar back in place.

All the way back to the house, walking through the wind, I was smiling. If the Mustang could get out and run, he would calm down. And if he calmed down, I was sure I could teach him to obey a lead rope. If I had even a week or two more, everything was going to be all right.

Every night after that, I went to my pantry a little earlier than usual, but not so much that the Stevenses noticed. Then, at about midnight, I would rouse myself and go to the barn. The stallion was skittish when I first let him out. But he began to expect me, and when I began insisting that he allow me to put on the halter before I let him out, he stood still while I slid it over his ears and buckled the throat latch. He was smart. He quickly learned that the halter didn't keep him from galloping until he felt better.

One night, I put the lead through the halter straps and gently tugged on it. He wanted to come out anyway, so he followed the pressure. I walked with him for a while, then let him loose in the aisle and stood aside. He bucked and galloped like a colt in an April pasture. It was wonderful to see him so happy.

CHAPTER NINE

❧ ❧ ❧

I wait every night for the sound of light footsteps
and the scent of crushed flowers. She is very young to
be a lead mare, but that seems to be her position.
She is kind and wise. I will follow her.

I was so tired all the time from staying up half the night with the Mustang that Mrs. Stevens finally asked if I was sick, but she had little time to worry about me. She was worried, constantly, about going west.

"Katie?" Mr. Stevens said at supper one night. I looked up at him. He was smiling. "Why don't you take the day off and go with Martha to the quilting party tomorrow?"

I stared at him. Mrs. Stevens always said that I was too young to go calling, that I couldn't sit still long enough—it had never once occurred to me that I would go this time.

Mrs. Stevens cleared her throat, and he turned to face her. "I've decided not to go," she said quietly. "I would feel terrible if your cousin came while I was gone and not here to welcome him."

Mr. Stevens didn't say anything for a long moment, then he looked at his wife. "Some people are coming to look at the farm tomorrow. I've decided, Martha. We are going west."

Mrs. Stevens lowered her eyes and said nothing. His sudden interest in her quilting needed no explanation now. He had wanted her out of the way for the day. And me as well.

"I expect you both to be cordial," Mr. Stevens said evenly.

"I will," Mrs. Stevens answered in a faint voice. Then she lifted her eyes. "I will honor my marriage and obey my husband," she said. "But I will never forgive you for this, Robert, and neither will Katie, when it comes to that. You will be taking her away from everything she knows, too." She gathered her skirt and stood up and left the room, leaving me staring at Mr. Stevens's flushed face.

"She's just upset about leaving her friends," he said in a low voice, talking more to himself than to me. "She'll get used to the idea."

"I want to go," I said timidly.

Mr. Stevens suddenly focused on my face, as though he had just realized that I was in the room with him. "You do?"

I nodded.

He smiled. "Well, that's fine, just fine." His voice was so reasonable that I smiled back at him. He seemed to take that as a sign to keep talking. "Mr. Peery and Mr. Gleason are going. And the Wilsons. The Themble family and maybe Mr. Dulin. And Hiram, I think."

Hiram was going? I was glad. But I remained still and silent. Mr. Stevens had never spoken this many words to me all at once. Ever. And he wasn't finished.

"We'll go by river from Muscatine to St. Louis, buy prairie-schooner wagons there, then go by road west to Independence. Everyone is using the schooners. They're half-size Conestogas, more or less." He raked his hair back with one hand, and I noticed deep circles under his eyes.

For a moment, I thought about telling him about the Mustang, how tame he was getting. But before I could, he reached out to pat my shoulder awkwardly.

"Martha will need your help getting ready to leave. We'll have to go as fast as we can once the farm is sold or we could end up overwintering somewhere. I don't want that."

I stared at him, my heart thudding inside my chest. It was real. We were going. I would make it to Oregon and find my family.

"We won't take much of this." He waved a hand vaguely at the whole room, the whole house. "Not past St. Louis, anyway. We can leave the blasted rugs with Martha's sister there."

I glanced around the room. The table had belonged to Mrs. Stevens's favorite aunt. The woodstove was something her parents had given her when she was first married. Her rugs were her pride and joy. The cupboard cabinets held dishes her father's mother had brought from England.

I had been so caught up in wanting to go that I hadn't thought about what it would mean for her—or myself, really. I could almost see my parents' home place from the hill. If I went west, I would almost certainly never see it again. The thought made me uneasy.

I am not sure when I noticed that Mr. Stevens was still talking. My thoughts were circling, tangling themselves into a knot so dense that his voice had literally faded.

"...homestead, which means that we have to build a dwelling of some kind on the land in the first year," he was saying. "The laws are very clear on that much, though they say there are people who couldn't manage it and have yet to be removed from their places."

"I heard Mr. Barrett talking about that," I said without thinking.

Mr. Stevens's face lit up. "You did?"

"You should be ashamed of yourself." Mrs. Stevens's voice was cold and flat.

I wrenched around, expecting her to scold me and send me to bed for speaking to her husband in such a familiar, disrespectful way. But she wasn't looking at me. She was looking at him.

Astonished, I watched her stare at him, and keep staring, until he turned away and walked out the front door into the darkness.

"Don't pin your dreams on any man," Mrs. Stevens said once he was gone. "Not a father, a brother, a friend, or a husband." She looked at me, and her eyes were hard as ice. "Just don't."

I nodded, not knowing how else to react.

"We cleaned the house for his cousin's visit?" she asked in a dull voice. "I never saw the letter." Then she laughed bitterly. "There is no cousin coming. He just wanted the house clean. He *planned* this, Katie."

"I'm so sorry," I said.

"Go read or something," Mrs. Stevens said in a low voice. "Just go on to bed and leave me alone for a while."

"May I go out to the barn?" I asked.

She waved one hand, nodding. "I don't care. Just go."

I went out the back door.

Mr. Stevens was standing on the front porch; I could see him in the moonlight. As I went up the hill, I heard the front door open and close and knew that he had gone back in to talk to his wife.

I went into the barn, glad to be away from them both. I led the stallion back and forth for an hour or more, then let him gallop. He wasn't nearly as desperate for every little bit of freedom now. He was calmer than he had ever been.

Shivering in the chilly evening, I put the lead rope on his halter and dared to open the barn door and walk him outside. For an instant, I was sure I had made a terrible mistake. His tossed his head and began to prance sideways, his neck arched. But when he felt me tug gently at the lead, he followed.

I led him in a circle around the ash tree, three or four times around, then halfway down the path and back up. Maybe it was the darkness that kept him from wanting to run away, but he didn't seem nervous or spooky at all, not even when the dogs barked a little. He kept lifting his head and taking great long breaths.

I led him down toward the house, along the lilac hedge at the edge of the yard, staying away from the dog yard, singing a little so the dogs could hear me and wouldn't bark again.

I thought about leading him right up to the door and showing Mr. Stevens how much he had learned, but I could hear them talking once I got close, so I turned and took the stallion back to the barn.

"We're going west," I told him when I put him back in his stall. "We're really going west!"

I slipped in the back door and tiptoed down the hall. They weren't talking anymore, and I didn't know if that was bad or good. I lay awake, dreaming about Oregon, about my real family, about how wonderful it would be to find them.

CHAPTER TEN

❧ ❧ ❧

The little one led me beneath the stars last night.
I hated coming back into the wooden box, but I followed
her. I will let her lead unless there is danger.

I woke the next morning, feeling uneasy. Mr.
and Mrs. Stevens were both silent at the breakfast table. Mrs. Stevens set her husband's plate in
front of him and walked back to the woodstove.
Mr. Stevens stared at the wall while he chewed.

I ate my oatmeal slowly, waiting for one of them
to speak, for them to at least pretend that things
were normal—they always had before when they'd
had an argument. But when I was nearly finished
eating—and they hadn't exchanged a single word—
I knew this time was different.

"When are they coming?" Mrs. Stevens finally asked. Her voice was so blunt, so heavy, that I flinched.

Mr. Stevens faced her. "First light, they said. They're staying with the Gibsons—she is Mary Esther's niece, I think. So they stayed there last night and—"

"Fine." Mrs. Stevens nodded sharply.

"They're the McCarty family from upper New York," he began again. "And they—"

"I'll be ready," she interrupted him, turning. "I had better dress properly. Katie can clean up breakfast."

I nodded, but I knew she didn't see me. I am not sure she cared whether or not her kitchen was tidy this morning. After they had both left the room, I rushed around, wiping up the table, the sideboard, setting the washed plates in the rack, putting the milk back in the cooler, wrapping the butter in its cloth.

When I heard the grinding sound of buggy wheels mixed with hoofbeats through the little kitchen window, I was just wringing out the dishrag. Breathless, I ran down the hall to get my shoes on.

The sun was sitting bright and round on the horizon. I was a half hour behind on my chores. I didn't think anyone else would care today, but Betsy would be wondering what was wrong.

I hurried out the back door, hoping the Mustang wouldn't be too nervous. He wasn't used to hearing strangers around the place. Halfway up the hill, Tiger pattered up behind me, running like wolves were after her. I noticed children's laughter and shouts mixed in with the sounds of the buggy coming up the road, and I knew what had scared her. Tiger wasn't used to the sounds of children playing. Mrs. Stevens insisted on my being quiet and polite—and I never had time to play.

I ducked inside the barn. The Mustang was standing with his head over the stall gate. I set the milk bucket down and ran to rub his ears. Tiger slipped beneath the lowest rail and lapped water out of his bucket. He barely noticed.

"Good for you," I said to him. "Maybe, after the McCarty family leaves, we can show Mr. Stevens how gentle you've gotten." I pushed his forelock out of his eyes and patted his wide forehead, tracing the swirl where his coat spiraled outward.

In the early light of the sun coming through the door, I could see the dust coming out of his coat. I had tried the currycomb weeks before, and he hadn't let me use it. But now maybe he would let me brush him—maybe I could get the last of the mats out of his mane.

"Tomorrow, I'll groom you," I promised him. "We'll wait until then to show Mr. Stevens how you let me lead you around."

An explosion of giggles made me turn. There were two girls standing in the doorway of the barn, both with curly fair hair. They were smiling at me, and my heart cracked open inside my chest. They looked enough like my little sister and me to be related. The younger one especially looked like Tess had, with a merry grin and pink, full cheeks.

Aching inside, I nodded politely at them and stepped back, picking up the milk pail. Tears were rolling down my cheeks, and I couldn't do anything to stop them. The sadness was as sudden and sharp as the night I had leaned against the Mustang's neck.

"We're Ruth and Mary," the older girl said.

I glanced back and saw her, pointing to herself

last. I tried to smile and couldn't. She looked seven or so; Mary looked about five.

Tess would have been six this year, I heard myself thinking. This summer, she would have turned six.

"My name is Katie," I managed. I didn't turn to look back at them. I knew if I did, they'd see my tears. How could I explain to them? I bit my lip. I didn't want to explain, I didn't want to have to tell them anything at all. They had no right to see me like this... to make me feel like this...

"Oh, what a pretty horse!"

I set down the bucket and whirled around in time to see a set of petticoats flouncing as little Ruth climbed the Mustang's stall gate and leaned toward him.

He snorted and lifted his head.

"Ruthie! Get down!" her older sister shrieked. The Mustang pawed at the dirt. Ruthie was hanging on to the rails, her skirts belling out as she leaned back. The stallion reared and pawed at the air, then kicked the back wall of this stall squarely. The sound of his hooves striking the wood rang out like a slammed door in a quiet house. Ruthie began to cry. The stallion reared again, his eyes rimmed in white.

"Get down!" I shouted.

The Mustang reared once more. Ruthie looked terrified, but she didn't climb down; instead, her crying turned into a wail.

"Get down!" her sister screamed.

Then Ruth leaned back even farther and I realized that she *couldn't* get down. Her skirts were caught on the rail. The Mustang had attacked the wood so many times it had splintered, and the long slivers of wood had snagged the fabric of her dress. The Mustang plunged in a circle, then rushed at the gate, his teeth bared.

Ruth screamed. It was a high-pitched, grating sound. The Mustang whirled away and squealed, slamming his back hooves into the planks again. I dropped the milk bucket and ran. The stallion spun in a tight circle, throwing clods of dirt into the air with his hooves.

As I ran, I heard adult voices, calling the girls' names, getting louder, but I kept my eyes on the Mustang. He was so scared, so trapped in the stall, I had no idea what he would do. He pawed at the ground, his nostrils flared wide.

"Get back from that horse!" Mr. Stevens shouted

as he ran through the open door. Just behind him was a younger man, his face twisted with worry. But I was closest, already reaching up just as the Mustang reared again.

I dragged Ruth off the stall gate. I heard her dress tearing, but I couldn't help it. The Mustang rushed the gate, his chest slamming against it, straining my makeshift repair on the latch—but Ruth was safe now, well out of reach. I set her down, and she ran to her father, crying hard.

Mr. Stevens strode to the tack room and came back brandishing the whip. He snapped it in the air, and the stallion retreated to the back wall.

"Wait!" I shouted at him. "Wait! I've been working with him and—"

The sound of the whip cut me off. Mr. Stevens's face was red, and his arm jerked up and down like a man working a pump handle. It was awful. The stallion squealed and shrieked, enraged, plunging in circles, trying to get away from the sting of the whip.

Ruth was pleading for Mr. Stevens to stop by the time he finally lowered the whip—we all were. I could only stand there, trembling, staring at the bloody welts on the stallion's face and neck.

"She scared him," I said, turning, my teeth clenched together. "I know she didn't mean to, but it wasn't his fault. She climbed up without asking, and all the shouting and crying scared him."

The Mustang had turned and stood facing the wall, his head angled just enough to see, his back hooves ready to smash anyone who came close.

"I'm so sorry," Ruth was saying over and over again. "I didn't mean to cause trouble!"

Mrs. McCarty took Ruth into her arms and spoke to her quietly while her father walked toward me. "We don't have any horses the girls can't pet," he said quietly. "Thank you so much for pulling her back."

I looked at him. I had no idea what to say. I couldn't think, and I didn't want to talk. I wanted them all to leave so I could take care of the Mustang, apologize to him, calm him down.

"I think it's best if we go look at the fields now," Mr. McCarty was saying. He lifted Ruth to his hip. Mrs. McCarty smiled at me, a tiny, unsure smile that faded when I didn't answer it.

Mr. Stevens turned on his heel before I could react, and the McCarty family followed him out the door.

"The horse is vicious," Mr. Stevens was saying over his shoulder. "I bought him from a crooked dealer."

I turned to the Mustang's stall and stood looking at him, tears streaming down my cheeks. I was desperate to explain to Mr. Stevens, to prove to him that the Mustang wasn't dangerous if no one startled him. And he could get used to more people; I knew he would. It would take longer now. He needed time and trust—not someone coming at him with a whip.

CHAPTER ELEVEN

※ ※ ※

I did not mean to hurt the young one,
only to scare it away. The older male with the stinging
stick can be glad there was stout wood between us.
If there had not been, he would have had to answer
an honest challenge, or try to run.

The McCartys walked every inch of the farm with Mr. Stevens that day. The two men strode around, picking up handfuls of the good, dark earth, peering down into the well, talking. Mrs. Stevens stayed in the house. Mrs. McCarty trailed along after the men, walking more slowly with her daughters holding her hands. I milked, then stayed in the barn for a while. The Mustang was pacing his stall, and he flattened his ears and tensed if I came close.

I finally took the milk to the house and got a soft cotton rag from the pantry and wet it in the basin. I ran back out to the barn. If Mrs. Stevens heard me come in—or go out again—she didn't shout at me for once.

It took a long time for the stallion to come to the front of the stall. He allowed me to touch the cool water to the whip welts, and, after a long time, he nuzzled my shoulder over the gate.

"It wasn't your fault," I told him over and over. "It wasn't your fault; it was mine. If I hadn't been crying, trying to hide it, I would have seen her in time." It was true, but he seemed to forgive me, and he still seemed to trust me. I was so relieved.

By late afternoon, when the McCartys finally left, the Mustang seemed calm again, but I wasn't. I watched Mr. Stevens and Mr. McCarty talking beside the wagon. Mr. McCarty nodded and extended his hand. Mr. Stevens took it firmly, and they shook—and I knew the farm had been sold.

When I finally went back into the house, it was nearly supper time. I found Mrs. Stevens in the kitchen, peering out the window, one hand hovering close to her face, even while she told me what to do. Her voice was quivering as though she might burst into tears.

I tried to think of something to say to make her feel better, but I knew there wasn't anything, not really. And I was afraid that anything I said would only turn her worry into anger—at me.

I went about my evening chores without trying to talk to her. She walked around each room a dozen times, her hand falling on one thing, then another. I knew what she was doing. She was trying to decide what to try to take with her and what to leave behind.

Mr. Stevens ate his supper in silence again that night. Mrs. Stevens barely looked at him—then went to bed early. He was gone when I got up the next morning, and we didn't see him all day.

That evening, Mrs. Stevens was quiet, but nervous as anything, turning to face the door every few minutes. I was anxious, too. Why hadn't he told us anything? Maybe I had been wrong about the McCartys buying the farm. Were we going?

I milked Betsy that night and talked to the Mustang for a few minutes, then raced back to the house. I had poured the milk out to cool, but before I could wash the bucket, I heard the buggy coming. I set it aside and ran for the front room.

Mrs. Stevens was already at the window. In the dusk, we saw two farm wagons, not the buggy. Mr. Stevens jumped down from one. It wasn't Midnight and Delia pulling it—it was a new team of dapple grays.

We heard him talking, and another man answered. I knew the voice. It was Hiram driving the second wagon—the buggy team pulling it. They both unhitched the horses and put them in the lower pasture. Mrs. Stevens finally moved away from the window and stirred the stew.

Mr. Stevens sat silently through dinner. Hiram kept shifting in his chair, like a man who would rather be somewhere else. Mr. Stevens finally finished his last bite of stew and dabbed at his mouth with his napkin. Then he cleared his throat. I saw Mrs. Stevens go stiff out of the corner of my eye. I held my breath.

"They bought the farm," he said evenly. He paused, then cleared his throat again. "Gleason and Peery want to travel together to St. Louis, and beyond. Themble, too. Dulin backed out. I think we may as well go with our neighbors. Hiram is joining us. We plan to leave Saturday at dawn."

Mrs. Stevens covered her mouth with one hand.

Mr. Stevens nodded as though she had spoken. "We'll take the two farm wagons. McCarty gave me an extra thirty dollars to pay for the iron stove and whatever else we can't carry. I've sold the buggy team to Hiram. I used Gleason's team to get the wagon home, but I want to use our oxen from here to Muscatine. No sense taking horses we won't use."

I blinked. Midnight and Delia belonged to Hiram now? Would he sell the Mustang, too? He had no idea how much I had worked with him, how much tamer he was now.

Mr. Stevens paused, and Mrs. Stevens didn't say anything. Mr. Stevens reached inside his coat. "Here's the list Barrett helped us write. We used the guidebooks, too." He look proud, smoothing out the paper on the table. I could see it from where I sat.

It began with "Thirty pounds beans, each person." The second entry was "Ten gills salt, per person," and so on. It wasn't all food I saw as he slid the paper toward his wife. There were entries for blankets, changes of clothing, how many pairs of shoes... it was a long list.

"If you can't follow it exactly," Mr. Stevens said, "come as close as you can and mark what we haven't got."

I stood up to lean forward so I could read the list better. "I don't have four pairs of shoes," I said quietly.

Mr. Stevens looked startled. "Well," he began, then he shrugged and looked at Mrs. Stevens. "We'll get some things in St. Louis."

I glanced down at my dress. It was ragged, and it was too small for me. Mr. Stevens complained every time he had to buy me a new one. I had wondered a few times if having to buy new clothing now and then was part of the reason they didn't want me to attend school.

"Go get some sleep, Katie," Mr. Stevens was saying.

I looked up at him. It was barely seven o'clock. I usually stayed up as late as they did—another hour at least.

He scowled. "Do as I say."

I stepped back from the table. I longed to stay up and hear about the journey. I glanced at Hiram. "I'm glad you're going," I told him.

He smiled at me and nodded.

"Katie!" Mrs. Stevens had raised her voice to the screechy pitch that made my teeth clench.

"Yes, ma'am," I said, and turned to go down the hallway. A movement caught my eye, and I glanced back. Hiram was staring at me. I smiled a little to let him know it was all right. I was used to them talking to me like this. It was worse when they were upset with each other.

I could hear Mr. Stevens start talking again—in a low voice—as soon as I opened my pantry doors. I lay on my pallet without undressing; I didn't even take off my shoes. I left the door ajar. I tried to listen, but I couldn't understand a word—they were talking too quietly.

I lay still for a long time, wishing I could slip out to the barn. I wanted to let the Mustang gallop, and I wanted to practice with the halter one more time. When I showed Mr. Stevens, I didn't want anything to go wrong.

I smiled in the dark. The truth was that I just wanted to tell someone the grand news. I was going west! My uncle Jack would be proud of me, proud of the Mustang. He would tell his friends to come over and see the amazing wild horse that his niece had tamed. His daughters would be a little jealous, but I would be so nice to them that they would understand how much it meant to me, how grateful I was and...

And I remembered the milk bucket. I had left it sitting just inside the back door, dirty. Mrs. Stevens was death on sour milk in the bucket on a normal day. Now she would likely willow-switch me. I stood up, glad I hadn't undressed. The voices in the kitchen had stilled. They had probably gone to bed.

I could wash the bucket without anyone hearing me, I was nearly certain. And even if they did hear, it would be better to admit I had forgotten it than to have Mrs. Stevens find it dirty.

I opened the pantry doors, then sat on my clotheshorse chair long enough to slide off my shoes and stockings. If I was barefoot, there was little chance they would hear me.

I went back up the hall, but instead of turning right into the kitchen, I stood silent, listening. They were in bed. I took another step and froze as I heard Mr. Stevens's voice.

"Martha, there are seven Scott County families going. Two want to drive their teams all the way to Independence. The others have arranged steamship passage to St. Louis as I have done."

He went on, and I heard him mention her rugs. I ran down the short hall to the back door while he was still talking. In the little bit of slanted light that shone into the hall from the kitchen, I lifted the bucket, careful not to let the metal bale clack on the wood. The basin was nice and full. I turned the bucket in a circle, using a rag to scrub the inside. Then I lifted it slowly, careful not to splash.

Relieved that I had managed to do the chore without being heard, I slid the bucket gently onto the table and turned to go back to bed.

Footsteps in the kitchen made me hesitate. Long shadows appeared on the hallway wall, and I ducked back to hide behind the table that held the basin.

"I want to talk to you," Mr. Stevens was saying quietly, "now that Martha has gone to bed."

I held my breath. They were coming down the hall, headed for the back door. They walked past me, then stopped.

"I haven't told Martha yet," Mr. Stevens whispered, "but I'm going to leave the girl in St. Louis. They have orphan homes there, lots of them."

My heart stopped beating, then started again, slowly, painfully.

Hiram didn't answer.

"And we may as well shoot the horse," Mr. Stevens added. "I can't sell it. Harris told everyone it attacked him, and the McCartys' story won't help. You can do it tomorrow. I'll take Martha and the girl with me to town to buy provisions."

He paused, and I could hear Hiram making his uneasy yes-no-maybe-so sound. I sank back against the wall, my dream of going west dissolving. An orphan home. The stallion dead. I pressed my lips together, holding back tears.

I could not let them hear me. I dared not. If Mr. Stevens knew I had overheard...

"The girl would do fine on the journey west, I think, and you can leave her with her uncle in Oregon," Hiram said. "The horse will gentle down, too, with travel and open air."

Mr. Stevens made an impatient sound. "The girl needs food and clothes and blankets and shoes, and we haven't money to spare, Hiram. The uncle never answered her letters—who knows if he's even alive? And the horse is dangerous. He could have killed the McCarty girl."

He was scared! I wanted to scream. *He wasn't trying to hurt anyone!* I bit my lower lip so hard I tasted blood, but I did not make a sound. I didn't dare. The Mustang's life depended on me now.

CHAPTER TWELVE

❧ ❧ ❧

*The sky smelled the same as it always had, a river
of smells, twisting and flowing. My hooves felt light as
moonlight on the earth. I had to slow my pace to follow,
but I was glad to do that much for the little one.*

I slipped down the hall to my pantry as soon
as they had gone back to the kitchen. I sat on
the edge of my pallet, thinking, shivering. I was
scared to death, but I had no choice. I had to take
the Mustang and leave, and I had to do it before
morning. Even if Hiram refused to shoot the
Mustang, Mr. Stevens would do it or hire someone else.

I heard Hiram leave for his shed. The lantern
light went out. I counted to a thousand. Then I
rose in the dark and lit one of my candle stubs.

Shivering and shaking, I used the pallet blanket to wrap my mother's book, the rest of my candle stubs, and the little striker I used to light them. It was Mrs. Stevens's striker and her blanket, and I made a vow I would send her the money to pay for both one day. I didn't want to be beholden to Mr. Stevens for anything. I found a piece of twine in the back room and tied the bundle tight at each end. Then I pulled in a deep breath.

I was so nervous leaving the house that my hands were shaking. The back door opened easily and without squeaking, and I ran, light-footed with fear, to the lilac hedge. I used a stick to dig up the little packet that held my father's silver shoe buckles. I slid it into the center of my blanket bundle, then crouched beneath the lilacs until I was sure no one had heard me leave the house.

Then I stood up and ran for the barn, slowing as I passed the dog yard to talk to them, letting them recognize my voice, then running on again.

When I saw lantern light shining from beneath the barn door, my stomach tightened. I thought Mr. Stevens had snuffed it. Maybe he had carried it out here? Was he going to shoot the Mustang tonight? Maybe Hiram had told him he didn't want to do it.

I sprinted up the hill and dropped my blanket bundle to jerk the door open, ready to shout, to scream, to fly at Mr. Stevens like a sparrow chases a hawk from its nesting tree. But it wasn't Mr. Stevens.

It was Hiram. He was standing near the Mustang's stall, and the Mustang had come within a few feet of him. Hiram took one look at my desperate face and nodded. "Mr. Stevens wants him shot."

I took a step closer, explaining that I had overheard everything.

Hiram grimaced.

I stood up straight. "I'm going to take the Mustang away from here tonight."

Hiram looked at me. "You are very brave."

"I'm scared," I told him. "I just don't have a choice."

Hiram shrugged. "But you can't ride him; you can't even lead him."

I set my shoulders. "Yes, I can. Stand over there and watch."

It took longer than usual, but I got the halter on the Mustang, then the rope. Hiram stood quietly, watching me lead him up and down the aisle. The Mustang was jumpy, but he stayed with me.

"The farm wagons..." Hiram said slowly. "One of them, I bought. And the farm team. I paid Mr. Stevens for the mares. He expected to load some of his things on my wagon. But now..."

I stared at Hiram, beginning to hope.

"Katie," he said slowly, "I don't like a man who would trick a girl and shoot a good horse. I can talk to him—"

"No matter what he says," I interrupted, "I won't believe him."

"Yes." Hiram waved one hand and nodded slowly. "How do we know what is truth with him?" He reached out and patted the top of my head. "We could both leave tonight."

I wanted to hug him, but I knew he wouldn't want me to, and it would startle the Mustang. So I led the stallion closer and put out my hand. Hiram extended his, and we shook like two grown men making a bargain.

"We take only what is ours," he said.

I nodded. Then I pointed at the halter. "That's not mine, and neither is the blanket or the flint

striker I took. I thought I would send them pay-
ment when I could."

Hiram nodded somberly. "You worked for them
three years for nothing but scant food and willow
switches. Will you work as hard on this long journey to the west?"

"Of course," I promised.

"Then I can leave a coin or two in the shed for
the halter and the blanket. Your work will pay me
back."

"Oh, thank you," I breathed. Then I shivered.
I pulled the hand-me-down jacket closer around
my shoulders and decided that it, and my raggedy
old dress, had been pay for my work, just like all
the bowls of cold boiled oats. And the Mustang?
Well, Mr. Stevens had decided to shoot him, so he
wasn't worth anything to him now anyway.

Hiram made his uneasy little sound, and I looked
at him. "The horse? You think he will stay by you,
follow a wagon?"

I nodded. It was true. It *had* to be true.

It took almost an hour to get the mares caught
and hitched up and all of Hiram's belongings
stacked on the flat wooden wagon bed. He had

been thinking about going west for a long time. He had water barrels and a little steel-bladed wheat grinder and a bag of beans and a kettle and other things I couldn't see well enough to identify in the dark.

We settled on my leading the stallion, walking just behind the wagon, so that he'd be less likely to bolt. Hiram tossed the dogs some hard bread rinds as we passed, so they didn't bark much. I held my breath all the way down the road, anyway, waiting for the sound of the wheels to wake Mr. Stevens, but it didn't. We made it.

We walked in silence that whole long night. Then, a half hour before sunrise, we passed my parents' farm. I couldn't see it in the dark, but I knew every inch of the place. I could imagine the house, the garden, the apple orchard my father had planted. And I knew exactly where the three little stones were that marked the graves. Hiram pulled the team to a halt. I heard him set the brake.

I walked the Mustang around the wagon and stood staring up the little farm road. I could see the shape of the house against the starry sky.

"I knew your folks a little," Hiram said. "From

church and raising a barn once for the Peerys. Your father was very proud of you. I know he still is." He paused, then said, "I would be."

I felt tears flood my eyes. The Mustang touched the top of my head with his muzzle. I reached up to press my hand against his neck as I stared up the hill at my parents' farm. My home.

"Good-bye," I whispered, and my throat ached. I wanted to go up the road, to touch the graves, to run my fingers over the headstones, to sit and remember all the mornings I had awakened on this farm, all the times I had played with my sister in the loft, all the happy years at the beginning of my life.

But I knew I couldn't—not without waking everyone who lived here now. They would ask questions; they would tell people we had passed; they might even feel they had to inform Mr. Stevens that I had taken his horse—and if they had dogs running loose, the Mustang might get away from me.

"Good-bye," I whispered a second time, with my eyes closed. "I love you."

"They'll watch over you wherever you are, Katie," Hiram said softly. "You can't leave them behind—

they live in your heart. But you can tell the place good-bye."

So I whispered it once more.

And after a long moment, we started off again. We walked at a steady pace, as we had all night. The sky turned from black to gray, then bloomed into roses as we walked on, heading away from the sunrise, heading west.